"Hav

Mor...
right?"

"Yes... ...someone understood her. "We just have to rearrange the furniture."

"I don't want anyone messing with my life," said Miles.

"Wait a second," Roxie said, holding up her hands. "I never agreed to any redecorating I don't like adjustments—even minor ones," said Roxie.

"Can't we just try it for a little while?" asked Sabrina. "C'mon, Roxie. It'll be fun."

"Don't I get a say? I never agreed to this!" said Miles. "These forces are powerful, and I don't think anyone should be trying to harness energy, messing with nature, or—"

"We could take a vote," Morgan said, cutting Miles off.

"Oh, why bother? You're all against me," said Miles. He threw up his hands and started to leave the room, but not before spinning around and offering his final afterthought. "But don't say I didn't warn you!"

Happy Birthday Rachael - 13th -
now you are a teen !!
more Sabrina Books following.
Enjoy these times they
come only once . Love
            mom
                    6/13/03

Sabrina, the Teenage Witch® books

Available from Simon & Schuster

. . . A GIRL BORN
WITHOUT THE FEAR GENE

FEARLESS™

A SERIES BY
FRANCINE PASCAL

SIMON
PULSE

FROM SIMON PULSE
PUBLISHED BY SIMON & SCHUSTER

3029

Have you read all of the books in the Harvey Angell trilogy?

Harvey Angell brightens up orphan Henry's life like a supercharged thunderbolt, and nothing will ever be the same again! But Harvey Angell's true identity is a mystery—one that Henry's got to solve!

While on a seaside vacation Henry discovers the ghost of an unhappy girl haunting his rental house. None of the lodgers is going to get any sleep until Henry and Harvey uncover the shocking secrets of Sibbald House.

Henry finds an extraordinary baby hidden in his garden—a baby with tiny antennae instead of eyebrows, and ears that look like buttercups! Henry's running out of time, and he has to find Harvey Angell before this mystery turns into a cosmic disaster.

Aladdin Paperbacks • Simon & Schuster Children's Publishing Division
www.SimonSaysKids.com

Sabrina The Teenage Witch®

Witch Glitch

Leslie Goldman

Based upon the characters in Archie Comics

And based upon the television series
Sabrina, The Teenage Witch
Created for television by Nell Scovell
Developed for television by Jonathan Schmock

Simon Pulse
New York   London   Toronto   Sydney   Singapore

First Simon Pulse edition April 2003
® & © Archie Comic Publications, Inc. © 2003 Viacom Productions Inc. Based upon the characters in Archie Comics. All rights reserved.

SIMON PULSE
An imprint of Simon & Schuster Children's Publishing Division
1230 Avenue of the Americas
New York, NY 10020

10 9 8 7 6 5 4 3 2 1

Library of Congress Control Number 2002107312

ISBN 0-689-85578-8

For Jim Margolis

Sabrina
The Teenage Witch®

Witch Glitch

Chapter 1

Saturday afternoons were Sabrina's favorite. Ever since she'd started college that term, Saturday afternoons had been her most relaxing and carefree time of the week. She usually managed to get most of her homework done by the afternoon, and the inevitable Saturday night party or date was hours away.

In this window of time, Sabrina reveled in the fact that she was cleared from any obligation and free to do whatever she wanted. The world was her oyster. The entire afternoon was hers for the taking, and this afternoon was incredible. On this beautiful spring day the sun was shining, the birds were chirping, and the flowers were blooming. Sabrina wandered around campus, breathing in the sweet smell of cherry blossoms from the trees. She swung by the library and returned some books, and then realized something: She was bored. It was so nice in the Mortal Realm, she didn't want to visit the Other Realm, just for a diversion, so Sabrina went home, hoping to find some company, but the off-campus house she shared with Roxie, Miles, and Morgan was empty.

Not in the mood to bike, skate, or read, Sabrina decided to drop by Hilda's coffeehouse to see what was going on there. Sabrina wasn't on the schedule to work that day, but she thought her aunt might need some extra help and, if not, the coffeehouse could be a fun place to hang out.

When Sabrina arrived that afternoon, she found the coffeehouse half empty. Two girls were contentedly sipping coffee at the table by the window. One guy with a long red ponytail, whom Sabrina recognized from last term's sociology class, was reading a book in an armchair and sipping a cappuccino. And an older couple was having a serious discussion on the couch. Their supersized lattes were half full. All of the empty tables had been bussed, and everything seemed to be in perfect order.

"Hey Sabrina," said Morgan Cavanaugh, who was reading a fashion magazine at the counter by the cash register.

Sabrina walked up to her housemate, resident adviser, and coworker. Morgan was bent over the magazine, her long red hair covering half of her face.

"Hey, Morgan, what's up?" asked Sabrina.

"Not much," she said, flipping back her hair and turning to the next page of her magazine.

"Looks kinda slow today," Sabrina said.

"Are you kidding," Morgan answered, pointing to the few patrons dotting the room. "It's been nonstop like this all day."

Sabrina looked around and asked, "Where's Aunt Hilda?"

"She's in back, doing inventory," said Morgan. She glanced over her shoulder and then leaned in toward Sabrina. Lowering her voice to a whisper, she said, "Do me a favor and don't tell her I'm reading on the job."

"Sure," Sabrina replied.

Morgan shook her head. "Hilda gets so bent out of shape when I do personal things during my shift. She's such a slave driver and so cheap when it comes to this place. I'll bet she's back there counting coffee beans."

Sabrina smiled. "Your secret's safe with me." She ducked behind the counter and then made her way into the back room. "Aunt Hilda? You here?" she called. "Do you need any help?" Once through the door, Sabrina stopped in her tracks.

Morgan was right: Hilda was very busy in the storage room. Except she wasn't doing the inventory—she was polishing her nails.

Hilda smiled up at her favorite and only niece and answered in her trademark high-pitched, squeaky voice. "No, I think I have everything under control here. Thanks for checking, though."

"Anytime," said Sabrina.

"Hey listen," said Hilda, lowering her voice to a whisper. "Don't tell Morgan I'm doing my nails. I have an image to maintain. And a big date tonight."

Sabrina suppressed her laughter and managed to repeat the words, "Your secret's safe with me."

"Good!" said Hilda. She did a quick point, and a nail dryer magically appeared. She looked down at her hand and gasped. "Oh no, I think I smeared the polish on my pinkie nail!"

"Do you still need to do inventory? Because I'm happy to help." Sabrina pointed her right index finger to her left hand and, within the blink of an eye, a palm-sized calculator appeared out of thin air.

"I already counted everything," said Hilda. "Twice."

"Do you need me to order more supplies or coffee?" asked Sabrina.

"Since when are you so concerned about this place?" asked Hilda.

"Oh you know. I'm just trying to help," she said.

"Right," Hilda said sarcastically. "So, what's the real story?"

"What do you mean?" asked Sabrina.

Hilda eyed her niece with suspicion and asked, "Are you bored?"

"Terribly," Sabrina admitted, hanging her head. She'd been feeling restless all day. It wasn't that there was any one thing wrong with her life, necessarily. It was more the fact that nothing was all that great.

"Want to do my toes?" Hilda waved the bottle of nail polish in front of Sabrina, who raised her eyebrows and shook her head vehemently.

"No thanks. I'm not that bored!" Sabrina looked around the room and suddenly noticed a bulletin board, filled with multicolored papers, hanging up above the desk. "Hey, speaking of boards, what's that?" she asked.

Hilda followed Sabrina's gaze and settled her eyes on the bulletin board. "Oh, I put that up the other day," she said. "Just because I own a coffeehouse in the community, everyone thinks I want to be a part of it! Ever since I lost that city council election, I'm done. Still, I've been getting a lot of flyers about local events—concerts, and lectures, that sort of thing—not to mention advertisements for baby-sitters, dog walkers, and bicycles for sale. I wanted to throw them all away. I mean, all of this information has got to be distracting to a potential coffee buyer. But Morgan talked me out of it. She thought it would be a good idea to display them all, so I picked up this bulletin board."

"That's a great idea," said Sabrina. "But I think Morgan meant that it would be a good idea to display these things for the customers."

Hilda looked at Sabrina blankly, asking, "Huh?"

"Like, outside," she suggested gently.

Hilda stared at the bulletin board and contemplated her niece's suggestion. "Maybe you're onto something there," she said.

"I think I am. And even better, it gives me something to do. I'll go hang this out front." Sabrina reached over and lifted the board off its hook on the wall.

A few moments later Sabrina found the perfect place for it next to the door. As she was straightening the bulletin board, one of the flyers caught her eye. The paper was pale blue, and the writing on it was done in silver metallic ink. She took it down and read:

6

*Feng shui may be the answer. But what's the ques-
tion? How is your health, love life, money flow,
friendships, and career? Want to improve them? It
could be as easy as lifting a finger or as moving an
end table. . . . Find out more Saturday at 4:00.*

Sabrina knew from experience that despite the
best intentions, lifting her finger didn't always improve things. So this really intrigued her. She
glanced up from the flyer and called out across
the coffeehouse, "Hey Morgan, have you ever
heard of feng shui?"

"Please don't distract me when I'm at work,"
said Morgan, who was in the process of reapply-
ing her lipstick, using the shiny surface of the cappuccino machine as a mirror.

"Sorry," Sabrina said as she walked out the
door.

Later that afternoon Sabrina headed to the feng
shui lecture, which was being held in the basement of the local library.

Once there, she took her seat among the crowd.
Sabrina didn't recognize anyone, but of the
twenty or so people in attendance, it looked like a
lot of them were college students. In the front of
the room sat a dark-haired woman who wore navy

slacks and a light gray silk blouse. She had a calm air about her. She cleared her throat, asked for everyone to settle down, and then introduced herself. "I am Bernice. I have been a feng shui consultant for ten years, and I am here to change your life." Her voice was so smooth, it reminded Sabrina of water cascading down over a rocky cliff.

Once the general murmur of the crowd had ceased, the woman continued.

"Feng shui is an ancient Chinese art. It's a powerful force that can be used to enhance your health, happiness, friendships, love life, career, and money flow. You think your life is going well now? Well, just wait and see how things can improve."

Wow, thought Sabrina. *Who doesn't want a better life?* Sabrina opened up her notebook and started taking notes.

Bernice went on to explain that feng shui is all about flow. Accordingly, where one lives and how one's furniture is arranged can have a direct effect on their luck, health, and general spirituality.

Sabrina was amazed by all of this. It had taken her a while to adjust to college life, but she had finally reached a balance between her schoolwork, her job at the coffeehouse and, more importantly, her social life. Now that she'd accomplished that, though, she was ready to make things even better. Any improvements made by simply moving around some furniture sounded like a snap.

Bernice explained that feng shui is a Chinese term, which translates into "wind and water." It's like yin and yang, and the opposing energies of day and night. "The energy takes five forms—fire, earth, wood, water, or metal," she said.

Sabrina wrote this all down. And by the time she finished taking notes on all of the aspects of feng shui, her hand was cramping up.

Bernice concluded forty-five minutes later, saying, "Good feng shui is based on the concept 'If you balance and harmonize the energy in your environment, you balance and harmonize yourself.' It all starts in the home."

Great, thought Sabrina. *You can never have too much harmony.* As she shook out her hand, she wondered how her housemates would react to this philosophy.

Her three housemates were terrific. Sabrina shared a room with Roxie, who had dark hair that reached down almost to her waist and a dark sense of humor to match. Roxie could be a bit gloomy sometimes, but once you got past her icy exterior she was a lot of fun. And after a few early mishaps, the two of them had become the closest of friends. Miles, who lived in the room next door, was a paranoid conspiracy theorist who had a million and one explanations for why, among other things, there was intelligent life on other planets. Sometimes he babbled on and on, but deep down Miles was a sweet, thoughtful, and intelligent guy, and Sabrina thought he was a good addition to the household. Then there was Morgan, their resident adviser. Morgan was a tad self-absorbed, more interested in her shoe collection than in anything going on in anyone else's life. But she was a lot of fun, and she always knew about the best parties.

Sabrina had no idea how Roxie, Miles, or Morgan would react to her new redecorating ideas, but there was only one way to find out.

"You guys, I have the perfect plan!" Sabrina yelled when she got home from the lecture.

"Great, I can't wait to hear it. Tell me about it as soon as my soap is over," Morgan said as she pointed the remote at the TV and turned up the volume. "Or better yet, just leave me a memo in my in box."

Sabrina walked over to the VCR and turned it off. "You don't have an in box, and you're watching a tape," she said.

"Hey," Morgan shouted.

"This is much more important than *Larry Loves Lisa*, I promise. Now, where are Roxie and Miles?"

"It's called *Live for Today*!" Morgan protested.

Sabrina marched toward Miles's door and knocked his secret knock, which seemed to change every month. "Are you in there?" she asked, rapping on his door for three short knocks, followed by two long knocks, and three more short ones.

"Hold on," Miles called through the door. "I'm just trying to figure out if there's a link between our most recent electricity bill and the earth's current position in relation to the constellations. I think I'm detecting a pattern."

"What?" asked Sabrina. That was her response to a lot of what Miles said.

Miles opened the door and peered out. He was looking particularly wide-eyed and frantic that day. "I've been up all night. I think I'm onto something this time." His dark brown hair stood out in five directions. This reminded Sabrina of the five forms of energy in feng shui.

"Hold your thought," she said. "I have great news."

Suddenly the door behind her opened, and Roxie peeked out, displaying her acute case of bedhead. "What's all this enthusiasm about?" she asked. "I'm trying to sleep."

"It's just after five o'clock in the afternoon," said Sabrina.

"Oh my gosh!" Morgan said, jumping up from the couch. "I have to get ready for the party tonight."

Sabrina spun around and said, "But the party isn't until after nine o'clock."

"Duh!" Morgan said, looking at Sabrina like she was missing something obvious. "There's so much to do between now and then. I have to file my nails and wash my hair. And I have no idea what I'm going to wear."

Morgan started to walk upstairs, but Sabrina pleaded with her. "Please, just hear what I have to say."

"Five minutes," Morgan said as she turned back around, sank into the couch, and looked at her watch. "Starting," she pointed at Sabrina, "now!"

"Thanks," Sabrina said, rolling her eyes. "Roxie?"

Roxie groaned but relented, sitting down next to Morgan.

Sabrina looked at Miles and tried to reason with him. "The electric bill isn't going anywhere."

"Okay," said Miles, sitting down on the other side of Morgan. "But remember I still need to find out which planet is tapping into our cable, too."

Sabrina pulled out her notebook and started. "Great. Thanks, guys. So, I just got back from this great lecture."

Roxie yawned. Morgan started brushing her long red hair. And Miles started picking at something on the carpet.

Sabrina tried to sound enthusiastic, hoping to peak their interest. "Have you guys ever heard of feng shui?"

"Yes, and it's frightening," said Miles. "Rasputin used to say that—"

"If you're ordering it for dinner, count me in," Roxie quipped, glancing at her watch.

Morgan actually perked up. "It has to do with decorating, right?"

"Yes." Sabrina was happy that someone understood her. "Feng shui translates into 'wind and water,'" she said, reading from her notes. "It's an ancient Chinese art. It's a powerful—"

"Blah, blah, blah," Morgan interrupted. "The clock is ticking, Sabrina. All I need to know I saw on the Style Network, and if that's good enough for them, it's good enough for me. As

13

long as it doesn't cost anything."

"We just have to rearrange the furniture." Sabrina paced back and forth as she surveyed their small living room. "Straight lines are bad, you see. We might have to redirect the energy flow by getting a mirror. Waterfalls are also very good to—"

"I don't want anyone messing with my life," said Miles. "This whole thing sounds kind of dangerous."

"Wait a second," Roxie said, holding up her hands. "I never agreed to any redecorating."

"Oh, come on," said Morgan. "Who couldn't use more mirrors?"

"We'd just need to move things around a little," Sabrina said to Roxie. "Minor adjustments, I promise."

"I don't like adjustments—even minor ones," said Roxie.

"Can't we just try it for a little while?" asked Sabrina. "It won't cost us anything. It's just rearranging what we already have." She planned on pointing up a few new things, but she'd just tell them it was stuff she had stored at her aunt's house. Everyone was pretty much watching every penny these days. "C'mon, Roxie. It'll be fun."

"I hate it when you say something's going to be

fun," said Roxie. "It's always followed by a w—"

"Does that mean you agree?" asked Sabrina.

"To try it, yes," Roxie said without enthusiasm.

"Woo-hoo!" Sabrina yelled, leaping up into the air.

"And there it is. Right on schedule," Roxie said dryly.

"This is gonna be so great!" said Sabrina.

"Wait a second, don't I get a say? I never agreed to this!" said Miles. "These forces are powerful, and I don't think anyone should be trying to harness energy, messing with nature, or—"

"We could take a vote," Morgan said, cutting Miles off.

"Oh, why bother? You're all against me," said Miles. "Just leave me out of it." He threw up his hands and started to leave the room, but not before spinning around and offering his final afterthought. "But don't say I didn't warn you!"

"That was easy," Sabrina said, collapsing in the easy chair and placing her hands behind her head. "I'm so glad you're all excited about this."

Roxie gave Sabrina her very unenthusiastic version of woo-hoo.

"Now where should we begin?" Sabrina wondered.

"Anywhere but my room or the bathroom,"

Morgan said as she shot up off the couch. "I've got work to do and I need my space."

Morgan was up the stairs in two steps.

"It's amazing how fast she can move when she wants to," Roxie observed.

"Okay, get up," Sabrina instructed. "I need to survey the room, see what we have to work with, consult my notes, make some sketches, determine—"

"Whoa, slow down there, Jackie Chan," Roxie said. "If you're going to be this whirlwind of activity, I'm going out for pizza. When do you think it will be safe to return?"

"Hard to say," Sabrina answered, already making mental calculations.

"I was afraid of that." Roxie tapped on Miles's door as she headed back to her room. "C'mon Miles," she yelled through the door. "We're temporarily vacating the premises while Grand feng shui Master Sabrina works her magic."

Miles grumbled something from behind his closed door.

"We're going for pizza, Miles," Roxie said knowingly.

"Be right out," he answered.

Good, Sabrina thought. *Then I really can work some magic!*

Chapter 2

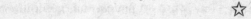

Sabrina wasn't the only person bored that Saturday afternoon and looking for a distraction. No, there was someone else.

That someone else was pretty and had long, straight, strawberry-blond hair. She was the same height as Sabrina and had Sabrina's same blue eyes. In fact, this someone had all of Sabrina's features. She even had a lot of the same expressions and gestures. To look at this person, one would think that she was Sabrina's twin. This would be technically correct, but it wouldn't be the whole story.

Katrina wasn't just Sabrina's twin. Katrina was Sabrina's *evil* twin. Stripped of her magic powers and doomed to spend an eternity in an Other Realm prison, Katrina Spellman was in a rotten mood, as usual.

That afternoon she was feeling particularly grim. The prison cafeteria had served Tater Tots and lizard's eyeballs for lunch. But out of thousands of prisoners, Katrina was the absolute last person in line, so by the time she was served, they were all out of lizard's eyeballs. Katrina hated Tater Tots. They were so pedestrian, so common. They reminded her of the Mortal Realm, which reminded her of Sabrina. Katrina didn't think it was fair that she was forced to spend an eternity in prison just because she was evil, while her twin Sabrina got to pop between the Mortal and Other Realms at the drop of a hat, just because she was good. According to Katrina's warped and twisted logic, such small details shouldn't have the momentous life-changing power that they did.

Katrina Spellman was thinking such thoughts as she paced back and forth in her cell, which she shared with Jezebelda, Zelda Spellman's evil twin. Instead of having neatly combed straight hair that fell to her shoulders, like Zelda's, Jezebelda had kinky blond hair that she teased into a puff high around her head.

"Hey Katrina, stop walking back and forth like that! You're making me dizzy and you're wearing out the floor!" Jezebelda said from where she sat on the bunk directly across from Katrina.

Katrina looked down at the concrete bottom of their cell to find that, indeed, she'd been walking for so long, she'd carved a half-inch dent into the ground.

"I'm just so bored!" Katrina yelled, stepping out of her path and throwing herself onto her own bed.

"Oh relax," Jezebelda said as she fluffed her pillow. "You must be able to find something to do."

"I already counted the bricks in our cell," Katrina said, kicking impetuously at the wall by her bed.

"At what time?" asked Jezebelda. The grout between the Other Realm cell bricks flashed on and off all day so that, half the time, the walls looked smooth. The bricks also expanded in the morning and contracted each afternoon, so counting each brick was no easy task.

"I counted from ten fifteen to eleven fifteen A.M.," said Katrina.

Curious, Jezebelda looked over and asked, "How many did you get?"

"Three thousand and four," Katrina said with a scowl.

"That's funny," Jezebelda said, scratching her head. "I counted three thousand and seven this morning. I wonder who's right." Jezebelda got up from her bed, walked to the back wall, and started counting bricks again.

Katrina turned over onto her stomach and buried her head under her pillow. She thought about her predicament and wallowed in self-pity. Not only was she stripped of her magic powers, cut off from the rest of society, and stuck eating starch-heavy meals, she was also forced to wear an ugly prison jumpsuit and share a tiny cell with Jezebelda, who had recently had a complete personality change, and in the process, had become a compulsive neat freak. Katrina could only chalk it up to some sort of shift in planetary alignment— or to too many Tater Tots.

The worst part about it was that Katrina had a hard time messing with people's lives from her vantage point. Sure, in the past she had managed to send an evil computer virus every now and again, but those days were over. Her computer privileges had been suspended.

"One hundred thirteen, one hundred fourteen," Jezebelda said as she dutifully counted bricks.

Katrina shot her cell mate an evil glare and shouted, "Can you keep it down, there? I can't even hear myself think!"

Jezebelda adjusted her tone to a whisper. "One

hundred fifteen, one hundred sixteen." Suddenly, she remembered something and spun around to face her cell mate. "Hey, things will get pretty exciting around here soon, remember?"

Katrina, sighing loudly and obnoxiously, asked, "Remember what?"

"Don't you read the prison newsletter?" Jezebelda's question came out more like an accusation, and Katrina didn't appreciate her tone.

"No," Katrina said indignantly. "I hate the newsletter. I hate this cell. I hate Tater Tots. And I hate everything about being here." She buried her head in her pillow to muffle her scream.

When Katrina was finished screaming, she sat up and asked in a hoarse voice, "Why, what did the newsletter say?"

"There's going to be a changing of the guard today," said Jezebelda. She turned back to the far wall. "Now where was I?"

"I think you're on one hundred fourteen," Katrina said with an evil grin.

"Thanks. Okay, one hundred fourteen, one hundred fifteen. Hey, wait a minute," Jezebelda said as she realized Katrina had tricked her. She threw her hands up. "Oh, never mind. I'll just wait until you're asleep again."

Jezebelda walked over to her bed and started

remaking it, creating perfect hospital corners, the folds of which were creased at exact forty-five-degree angles.

Katrina glared at her fastidious cell mate and got more and more upset, finally having to ask, "Oh, what's the point of that?"

Jezebelda ignored her and fluffed her pillow again.

"You do that eight times a day," Katrina whined.

"Nine times on most days, and ten on Tuesdays." Jezebelda held up her hand and started counting off on her fingers. "I count bricks on Saturdays, Mondays, and Wednesdays; I file my nails on Sundays and Thursdays; I remake my bed at eleven thirty and four o'clock . . . I think that having a routine is healthy. Maybe you should try it."

"Sure, except I hate routines," Katrina said, rolling her eyes. "When's dinner?"

"At seven thirty, just like it is every day," Jezebelda reminded her.

"I hate eating at seven thirty," Katrina shouted into her pillow, and then punched it with her fist. "I don't understand why we have to eat at the same time every day!"

"Because I said so!" boomed a loud and vicious voice from above.

"Who was that?" Katrina asked, looking around, wide-eyed.

Jezebelda pointed up to a speaker and a small camera in one corner of the cell. "It must be the new prison guard. Careful what you say," she whispered with a wink.

Katrina marveled at the small silver lens that seemed to follow her every movement and asked, "What is that thing and how long has it been watching us?"

"If you read the newsletter then you'd know what that is," Jezebelda said, chuckling.

"What is it?" Katrina snapped.

"It's a Webcam. A new policy from ORPS." Jezebelda glanced at Katrina and wondered if her cell mate knew that ORPS stood for Other Realm Prison System. "They cut down on prison guards because now they can watch us from a central location."

"But when did this happen? And why didn't I notice it before?"

"Max was just installed the other day."

"Max?" Katrina asked.

"I named it Max." Jezebelda beamed up at the camera and gave it a little wave. "Doesn't he look like a Max?"

"Sure," said Katrina.

"There are going to be a lot of changes around here," Jezebelda said, stepping into the groove Katrina had made and pacing back and forth. "They're redoing the entire computer system, updating the files, installing new software."

"Really?" asked Katrina.

"Do you ever pay attention to what's going on here?" Jezebelda asked impatiently.

"Why? What's the point?" Katrina asked as she walked over to the front of the cell and clutched two of the bars.

A new prison guard was passing by the front of their cell block. Katrina eyed her. At seven feet tall, the new guard was beautiful. Her hair was gold with a shock of bright pink, and her eyes were round and silver like a pair of shiny dimes from the Mortal Realm.

Katrina studied her and, in a voice full of bitterness, asked, "I thought *you* were replaced by Max."

The guard walked up to Katrina's cell, peered in, and asked, "Who's Max?" Her voice was deep and bearlike.

"Sorry," Katrina said, although she didn't sound like she meant it. "I mean the Webcam. I thought technology was taking over. You know, replacing the living and breathing—that type of thing."

The guard looked at Katrina. She was so close,

Katrina could see her own reflection in the woman's eyes. "They still need us guards to do backup. You can't trust computers for everything, you know."

"I know," Katrina said earnestly. "I couldn't agree with you more. I sent a computer virus down to the Mortal Realm once. I was intent on ruining someone's life, and it *so* didn't work out the way I had planned."

"We can't forget that computers make errors." The guard opened up her notebook and looked inside. Katrina noticed that, instead of hands, the guard had bearlike paws, the fur of which was Day-Glo orange. "They installed some new software, and there was a glitch in the system." The guard looked at Katrina. "Anyway, it looks like a lot of prisoners are being held here for no reason."

"Really?" Katrina said, trying to figure out how she could work this new bit of information to her advantage.

"Yes, a lot of our prisoners just don't belong here," said the guard in a husky voice.

Katrina glanced over her shoulder and was relieved to find Jezebelda folding and then refolding her spare prison uniform. "I couldn't agree with you more," Katrina said, suddenly very interested in what the guard had to say.

The guard looked from Katrina's cell—number 8—to her notebook and back again. She leaned toward Katrina so close, Katrina could smell pepperoni pizza on her breath.

Katrina's stomach growled. Oh, what she wouldn't do for some pepperoni pizza! But they didn't serve that to prisoners.

"Are you Katrina Spellman?" asked the furry-pawed guard.

"Yes, I am," said Katrina.

The guard eyed Katrina suspiciously. "Well, it says here that your term is up."

"What? Really?" said Katrina. She looked back at the Webcam, and suddenly everything came together.

In updating their files, the bureaucracy of the Other Realm Prison System must have made a mistake. Good old ORPS!

As the truth sank in, she changed her tune. "Of course," Katrina said sweetly. She smoothed down her hair and said, "I knew that. I was just waiting for you to get here. I don't belong here any longer."

Jezebelda stood up suddenly and asked, "What's going on here?"

The guard took a giant key off her ring—not an easy task, considering her lack of opposable thumbs—and told Katrina, "You're free to go."

"Really?" Katrina said, jumping up and down. "I mean, of course. Of course I'm free to go. Uh, go where?"

"Go to Neptune, I suppose. That's where you were living, right? That's what the file says, anyway."

Katrina smiled. As if she were from Neptune! She'd been there once, on a package weekend vacation, and had found the place to be dreadful: tacky and full of neon signs and strip malls. But she didn't say that, now. "Neptune. Oh, it will be so nice to be home."

The guard began to unlock the prison cell door.

"Hold on a second," Jezebelda said, her protests drowned out by Katrina's squeals of excitement.

"It's been so long since I've been there!" Katrina exclaimed.

"Someone tell me what's happening," said Jezebelda. "I think there's been a mistake."

But the guard wasn't listening to her. She was entering something into her handheld computer system.

Jezebelda tried to approach the guard, but Katrina pushed her back down, whispering, "Keep quiet and I'll make it worth your while. If you don't say anything, I'll send you some Oreos from the Mortal Realm."

"If you think bribes are going to work with me, young lady . . ." Jezebelda stood up and put her hands on her hips to finish her thought. "You are absolutely correct!"

"Great," Katrina said, stepping out of the cell.

As Katrina walked toward the glowing exit portal, she nervously glanced at the guard, still not quite believing her luck.

"There's only one catch," said the guard.

"Catch?" Katrina said with a huff, trying not to sound as if she'd just been let out due to a mistake.

"Nothing big," said the guard. "I just need to warn you—you've been stripped of your powers for so long that they may be a little rusty."

"Oh," Katrina said, relieved. "Of course."

"Here," the guard said, pulling a can of oil out of her pocket and shaking it.

Katrina walked closer, eyeing the can suspiciously.

The guard sprayed her for a few seconds, saying, "This should help, but it's no cure-all. Be careful out there."

"Okay, thanks," said Katrina. "Can I go now?"

As the guard slid the door shut again, Jezebelda

called, "Make sure you get Double-Stuffed. And if you can find the chocolate-covered ones, all the better!"

The guard pressed a button on her computer, and the portal sucked Katrina into it. She was sent to Neptune in the blink of an eye, but Katrina didn't plan to spend very much time there. Neptune had changed a lot since Katrina had been there five years before. She didn't have the right clothes or the right shoes. And she certainly didn't have the right hairstyle. Luckily they had plenty of strip malls. But Katrina couldn't execute her plans wearing a prison jumpsuit and sneakers. She pointed up a credit card and started shopping. She'd have to look perfect for everything to work.

The next morning after a shopping spree and long rest in a soft Neptunian cloud bed, Katrina headed straight for the Mortal Realm—to Adams College, in Boston, Massachusetts, to be more specific.

She hadn't seen her twin in a while, and Katrina thought it was time to catch up.

She found Sabrina's house with little trouble. Looking through a window, she saw that her good twin was talking to three people. Two were young women. One of them had long red hair, and the other had dark brown hair. A boy was there, too.

He had dark, very messy hair. Katrina leaned in closer to try to listen, but she couldn't quite make out what they were saying. Deciding to make use of her newly returned powers, Katrina shrank herself down to the size of a peanut and pointed herself behind a side table lamp—a perfect position to eavesdrop.

Sabrina paced back and forth in front of her housemates on Sunday morning. She had gathered them together bright and early—by college standards, anyway. It was 11:30, and they were all grumbling. Roxie was still in her pajamas. Or, to be more accurate, she was in old sweatpants that Sabrina assumed were pajamas—she could never quite tell, with Roxie. Miles was dressed, but his hair was even more messy than usual, and Morgan was sipping coffee grumpily.

Sabrina, of course, was too excited to notice their lack of enthusiasm. Her voice was bright and cheery. "So, I've been reading about this all morning, and there are six aspects to the art of feng shui, not to be confused with the five forms," she told them.

"Sabrina, I'm not really up for math right now," Roxie said, and yawned.

Sabrina ignored the comment and forged ahead.

"Normally, the house is supposed to be arranged according to the head of the household. But since we don't really have a head of the household, I thought that—"

"Excuse me, question," Morgan said, raising her hand as if she were in class. "As the RA, I believe that I'm the head of the household and therefore—"

"Come on, Morgan," Miles said in a weary voice.

Morgan glared at him, saying, "What? I am the head of the household and I'm the one who's most excited by this, so I think it's just natural that I should benefit the most."

"There is a way we could all benefit," said Sabrina.

"Never mind everyone," said Morgan. "How can it benefit me?"

Sabrina flipped open her notebook and said, "I thought we could do our rooms to enhance whatever aspects are most important to us. There are six areas of one's life that feng shui can improve. I think we should decide what we want for the common areas and rearrange things accordingly. What do you guys think?"

Sabrina got blank stares from Roxie and Miles, but Morgan piped up, asking, "What are the aspects? And is there one that will improve my wardrobe?"

"Nothing could improve your wardrobe," Roxie said snidely. Looking at Morgan, who was wearing a light blue robe with a hot pink faux fur collar, she added, "The problem is your taste."

"You should talk. I've never seen you in anything but those putrid green army pants!" Morgan answered.

Miles, his nasal voice sounding particularly whiny that morning, quipped, "I just want you all to know that I still object to this very strongly. I just came out here to get some fresh air. I'd be in my room, except my latest chemistry experiment exploded and I have to wait for it to dry and . . . and . . ." Miles couldn't finish his thought, because he sneezed.

"Miles, are you getting a cold?" Sabrina asked, who, unlike her other housemates, was sincerely concerned.

"It's just allergies." Miles grabbed a tissue and blew loudly. "Or maybe a cold, or maybe some rare tropical disease." Miles was starting to scare himself.

Sabrina clapped her hands together and said, "Hey, that's perfect. Why don't you focus on health?"

"Huh?" Miles said, bewildered.

"Health is one of the elements of feng shui. Just

try it, okay? It can't hurt. How many times a week are you at your doctor's office?"

"Which doctor?" Miles asked.

"How many do you have?" Roxie asked, looking incredulously at Miles.

He answered too softly for anyone to hear.

"What?" asked Sabrina.

"Six," he whispered. This time his voice was audible—but only barely.

Morgan gasped. "Unbelievable!"

"What?" said Miles, shrugging. "That's an improvement. I used to have eight."

"So maybe we can cut you down to only five, if this works out," said Sabrina.

Miles looked at her suspiciously and weighed his options. "Okay, okay," he said, finally relenting. "You can do this feng shui thing on me. But only if it gets you off my case."

"Great," said Sabrina. "Glad you're so enthusiastic and open to this. Okay, that's one." She checked health off her list and wrote Miles's name next to it. "Now we have friendships, general happiness, love life—"

"Love life, right here!" Roxie said, raising her hand and pointing down at herself.

"Okay, great," said Sabrina.

"What's all this about? I thought you didn't

want any part of this," said a very surprised Morgan.

Roxie started to blush, but admitted, "I have a major crush on this guy in my art class. His name is Justin Spencer."

"Love life—Roxie," Sabrina said, adding it to her list. "That leaves money flow. What do you think, Morgan?"

"I could always use some more money flow," said Morgan, who unhappily had to get the job at Hilda's coffeehouse after her parents cut off her credit. "Put me down for that. And I'll take twenty dollars right now."

"It's not like we're installing an ATM in the kitchen," Sabrina said as she wrote down Morgan's name after money flow.

"No, but not a bad idea," Katrina said softly from her hiding place behind the lamp. Katrina pointed up a notebook of her own. She copied down: Miles=health. Roxie=love life (Justin Spencer, art class), and Morgan=money flow.

"What are you going to focus on?" Roxie asked Sabrina.

"I think I'll do career," Sabrina said, writing down her own name. "I don't want to work at Hilda's coffeehouse forever. I think journalism is the path I want to go down, but I'm not positive.

Maybe some redecorating will help me figure out what I really want to do with my life."

"So now what do we do?" asked Morgan.

"Let's rearrange the living room furniture," said Sabrina. "I drew up a little sketch based on the principles of feng shui. You see, straight lines are bad, so we should change the angle of the couch. Otherwise, it cuts off the flow of the entire room."

Sabrina, Miles, and Roxie lined up along the couch and started to push it at an angle. Morgan watched them.

"I can't believe I was talked into this," said Miles.

"Tell me about it," Roxie said as she alternated between grunting and pushing.

Morgan sat down in the easy chair and picked up a magazine.

"Morgan, want to help here?" asked Sabrina.

"Not really," Morgan said matter-of-factly.

When she noticed her housemates staring at her she ran upstairs to her room and slammed the door before anyone could argue with her.

Meanwhile, Miles tried pushing the coffee table, but it wouldn't budge. "Ow! I think I slipped a disc in my back!" he yelled as he keeled over onto the floor.

"From moving the coffee table?" Roxie said,

picking up a corner with one hand and dragging it across the room.

"I twisted wrong," grumbled Miles. "Now I'll be back to seven doctors. So far this is working like a charm, Sabrina."

Tired of watching the mortals, and afraid they might next try to move the lamp on the side table, Katrina pointed herself back outside. Because she was still in miniature, the soft grass cushioned her fall and she landed with a quiet thump. Suddenly Katrina heard a loud flutter of wings. She looked up and gasped, then turned herself back into human size just in the nick of time. A small sparrow had been about to make her lunch!

She shooed the surprised bird away, brushed herself off, and then reached into her back pocket to get her notebook. She couldn't find it at first, and then she realized why: It was still tiny. She picked it up between two fingers and studied it. The notebook was the size of a small stud earring. Katrina tried zapping it again, but the notebook wouldn't budge. The furry-pawed prison guard had warned her that this type of glitch was bound to happen from time to time. Katrina tried to look on the bright side: At least she was able to turn *herself* back into the right size.

Still, she wanted to be careful. She told herself

she'd only use her magic when absolutely necessary. No need to accidentally mess up something that could tip off Sabrina she was here. This feng shui redecorating thing was the perfect way to cause a little mischief in Sabrina's perfect life. Now that she knew her housemates' weaknesses, she could do everything in her power to exploit them. And as for Sabrina—Katrina was an old pro at wreaking havoc on her Goody Two-shoes twin. She smiled at the prospect of having some evil old fun for the first time in a long while.

Chapter 3

"Now let's see . . ." Sabrina paced back and forth in her bedroom on Monday morning, thrilled that she finally had time to "fix" her life. Sunday had been devoted to sprucing up the living room, and she'd had to pull a shift at Hilda's coffehouse that night. Between that, finishing up a term paper for her history class, and writing up her biology lab, Sabrina was left with no time to redecorate her bedroom. But now she had the perfect opportunity. Roxie was in class for the next few hours, and she had given Sabrina the go-ahead, albeit reluctantly, to "feng shui" their room.

Sabrina picked up her new feng shui manual, which contained details only glossed over in Saturday's seminar. She sat down at her desk and read from the chapter on bedrooms.

"When in bed, it's important to see who's

entering the room, directly or through a mirror. Hmmm." She pulled her hair up in a loose pony-tail, secured it with a tortoiseshell clip, and continued to read. "At the same time, of course, you can't have the foot of the bed facing the door, or the headboard touching the wall. But part of the bed should touch the wall."

Sabrina looked over at her own bed. She scooted the headboard away from the wall and tried to figure out how to get one side of it to touch the wall. Between hers and Roxie's furniture, there just wasn't much room. Standing over her bed and staring at the multicolored spread, Sabrina thought very hard about how to fix this problem, but she was soon interrupted.

"What in heaven's name do you think you're doing?"

"Ah!" Sabrina screamed. There on her windowsill was Salem Saberhagen. Salem looked like an ordinary black cat, but he was so much more. In the past, Salem was a warlock who had gotten in trouble for trying to take over the world. As punishment, he was sentenced to serve one hundred years in the Mortal Realm in the form of a house cat. He lived with Hilda and Zelda, but visited Sabrina whenever he got bored or was in the mood to cause trouble, which was fairly often.

"Salem, you scared me," Sabrina said, sinking down onto her bed.

"Then my work here is done," Salem said, looking around and noticing the notes and book spread out on Sabrina's desk. "What are you up to?"

"I'm redecorating."

"Interesting look," Salem said snidely, observing the furniture in various states of upheaval.

"It's not like that," said Sabrina. "I went to the most amazing lecture the other night. It was on the art of feng shui. I thought my life could use a little fine-tuning, so . . ." Her voice trailed off because Salem was sighing and shaking his head knowingly.

"Feng shui," he said. "I think I was there once. Little bar in downtown Hong Kong, right?"

"Feng shui means 'wind and water,'" said Sabrina. "It's a philosophy, a way of life, not a place." She pointed and conjured up a small fountain in one corner of the room. Wrinkling her nose, she pointed again to move it over a couple of inches.

Salem climbed down from the windowsill and hopped up onto Sabrina's desk, pushing over her feng shui manual, which was in his way. The book crashed down to the floor, much to Sabrina's annoyance. Salem, however, ignored it. "You say philosophy. I say . . . what's for lunch? I'm thinking Chinese."

Sabrina picked up her book and gave him a look. "Where do you think I should hang this mirror?"

"What mirror?" asked Salem.

"Oh, I forgot!" Sabrina said as she pointed her finger at her bed. A large rectangular mirror appeared. "I've got to hang it somewhere so that both Roxie and I can see the bedroom door from our beds."

"So what's wrong with your life, anyway?" asked Salem. "You've got your powers, you've got your thumbs, what more could you want?

Sabrina shrugged. "I don't know, exactly. It's not like there's any one thing wrong. I just want things to go . . . better." She pointed up a bonsai tree and asked, "Do you think this is overkill?"

"Will you scratch behind my ears?" Salem asked, clearly uninterested in Sabrina's dilemma.

She looked at him impatiently. "I have a lot of work to do, so if you'll excuse me."

Salem took this opportunity to leap from Sabrina's desk onto her bed—even though she had told him a number of times to stay off. "So is there any money to be made on this, and how can I get in on the action?" he asked, looking up and flashing her a grin that was all fangs.

Sabrina sighed and scratched Salem's ears.

"Ooh!" said Salem. "Yeah! That feels good. A little to the left."

Sabrina had to smile. Salem could be a real pain sometimes, but he was also one of her best friends. *Friends!* Roxie would be back from class soon, and Sabrina wasn't anywhere close to being finished with the room.

Sabrina stood up. Salem had just about dozed off from the ear massage. The lack of scratching snapped him out of his blissful state. "Hey, why did you stop?" he asked.

"Time for you to go, Salem. I've got to finish this and get to class."

"Go right ahead." He yawned and stretched out on the bed. "Don't mind me."

Sabrina looked at him disapprovingly. "No really, Salem. I've got work to do."

"So who's stopping you?"

Sabrina raised her finger and said, "Don't make me use this. You know how you hate to be zapped."

Salem jumped up. "All right, already! You don't have to tell me twice. I'll catch you later." Salem leaped through the open window and landed on the grass outside.

He didn't notice, but when he walked by the low hedges underneath Sabrina's window, there was someone hiding in them. That someone was Katrina. She suppressed her very strong urge to pull Salem's tail and tried to concentrate on Sabrina. She was already on edge, already kind of cranky. Going from ORPS to Neptune to the Mortal Realm in such a short period of time had left her with a nasty case of jet lag.

"Now, back to work," Sabrina said, glancing down at her manual. "The color of one's bedroom should complement a personal element. Fire is green. The earth is red. Metal is yellow. Water is white. And wood is blue." Sabrina consulted the chart in the back of the book.

Katrina watched her from the window and whispered, "Roses are red, violets are blue, you're my good twin, but I hate you!"

Sabrina looked up. *What was that?* she wondered. She looked out her window, thinking that it was Salem, but the cat was gone.

The bushes shook slightly, but Sabrina figured it was because of the breeze. She went back to deciding her personal feng shui element and asked, "Hmm, now what am I?"

"You're horrible!" Katrina hissed, unable to control herself.

Assuming that Salem was playing tricks on her, Sabrina frowned, walked back to her window, and slammed it shut.

Sabrina read that a person's element depended upon the year and time of day of their birth. Determining that she was a wood and Roxie was a metal, Sabrina pointed her finger at the wall above her bed and zapped it blue. She pointed at the wall by Roxie's bed, and it went from white to yellow in the blink of an eye.

Sabrina blew on her finger and smiled. She'd tell Roxie she'd painted the walls, and after class she'd dab some yellow paint on her ear and put a small splash of blue in her hair. Just to be on the safe side, she zapped up a faint "new paint smell" to fill the air. *It's good to be a witch,* Sabrina mused as she slightly rearranged the beds and then finished by hanging the mirror because, according to feng shui, it was important to see who was entering her room, and her life. Smiling in satisfaction at the finished room, Sabrina was ready for a change, and excited to see what would happen.

Katrina climbed out of the bushes, saying, "Sabrina thinks that she can make her perfect life even better by moving around the furniture. I'll show her what can really happen."

The evil twin walked off to the campus of Adams College. She was itching to start some mischief, but first she had to eat. Katrina's stomach was growling loudly.

Her first stop was the dining hall. She'd noticed students just showing their I.D.s and not having to pay for their food. She quickly pointed up a card that said SABRINA SPELLMAN and got in line. She piled her tray high with three doughnuts, two cups of coffee, a bagel with extra cream cheese, a heap of bacon, three large spoonfuls of scrambled eggs, a large stack of pancakes, some French toast, a glass of grapefruit juice, a glass of orange juice, and a glass of tomato juice. "These Mortal Realm breakfasts are great!" she said to herself. "Nothing like prison food." She surveyed the breakfast buffet and added some hash browns to her plate. Condiments next: Katrina balanced mustard, ketchup, relish, mayonnaise, salt, and pepper onto her tray, then sat down at an empty table.

Katrina looked at her fork and then at her plate piled high with food. "I just wish the utensils here weren't so small." She glanced around. There were a lot of college students in the cafeteria, but none of them were paying her any attention, so she pointed her finger, and her fork doubled in size. She pointed it again, wanting the fork to triple in size, but nothing happened.

"Drat!" she said, pointing her finger and trying again, shouting, "Double drat!" when the fork shrank back down to its original size.

Katrina finished her breakfast and burped the daintiest burp she could muster—which caused some heads to turn. Then she wandered around campus, trying to advance her plan.

She pulled out her trusty notebook, which, since her magic wasn't working so well, was still the size of an earring. Katrina pointed and tried to enlarge it again, but nothing happened. She squinted, trying to read the very, very fine print, but found she still couldn't see it.

Frustrated, Katrina wandered around campus, stopping in the student bookstore. She walked up to the first clerk she saw and asked, quite rudely, "Does this place have magnifying glasses?"

"Sure, right over there," the clerk said, pointing to a wall on the far left side of the store that was filled with pens, pencils, Hi-Liters, scissors, staplers, and other school supplies, including a decent selection of magnifying glasses.

Katrina picked up the first one she saw and studied her list. She had to squint, but she could finally make out the writing with the help of the lens. She started to walk out of the store when the security guard stopped her. "Hey, are you going to pay for that?" he asked.

Katrina looked in her pockets and realized she didn't have any money. "Actually, no," she said, and bolted out of the store.

She ran all the way to the other side of campus and then collapsed against a tree. Trying one last time to zap her notebook back to its normal size, she found that this time it worked.

"Ah-ha!" yelled Katrina. She threw the magnifying glass over her shoulder, and it hit someone on the head.

"Ow!" yelled a scruffy-haired Adams student who had thought he'd found a quiet place to study.

"Sorry," said Katrina, who then mumbled, "Mortals," under her breath. She looked down at her notebook, focusing on one entry. Sabrina=Career. Katrina already knew what she was going to do.

"Which way is the, uh, what's it called?" she asked the student, interrupting his reading once more.

He looked up from his book and asked "The what?"

"The place where I can go to drop Sabrina's—I mean, drop all of *my* classes," said Katrina.

"You mean the registrar?" asked the student.

"Yes, the registrar," said Katrina. "Where is it?"

The student pointed to a large brick building in the northeast corner of campus, and Katrina cackled.

"Shh!" he said again.

Katrina growled at him. She made her way across the large quad on her way to the registrar's building, but was soon interrupted.

"Hey, Sabrina!" Roxie ran up to the person she thought was her friend and housemate. "What kind of damage have you been doing back at home?" she joked.

"Uh . . . oh, nothing. What do you mean? Who did you see and what do you know?" She narrowed her eyes at Roxie.

"Oh, I was just kidding. I'm surprised to see you on campus, though. I figured you'd be busy redecorating." Roxie glanced at her watch, adding, "I thought you didn't have class for another hour."

"I don't," Katrina said, her voice bristling with anger. "But I don't need *you* to tell me that."

At first Roxie didn't know how to respond to that comment. It was so out of character coming from her perpetually perky housemate. Roxie was the one who was usually hostile. "Geez, what's wrong with you?" she asked. "Are you feeling unbalanced? Did you trip over the couch after we moved it or something?" Roxie couldn't help but make fun of Sabrina's new hobby.

"No," said Katrina. "It's nothing." Then, she thought of something. "Hey, are you still interested in that mortal—I mean, that guy—from your art class? What was his name again?"

"Justin? Yeah, of course," Roxie said, lighting up. "Why?"

"I, uh, it's part of the whole feng shui thing," said Katrina. "What does he look like?"

"He's about five foot nine inches, with blue eyes the color of the Mediterranean, and the tan of a Greek god. He's also got these amazing hands. . . ." Roxie's eyes glazed over as she thought about Justin.

Meanwhile, Katrina took notes in her spiral notebook.

"How do his looks figure into the furniture thing? What are you writing down?" Roxie asked, suddenly curious.

"Nothing," Katrina said, putting her notebook away.

Roxie readjusted her backpack, pushing it up further on her shoulder. "Do you want to grab a coffee? I have fifteen minutes before my next class."

"No way," said Katrina.

Roxie shook her head. "Aren't we a little grumpy this morning?"

"Sorry," Katrina said, not wanting to blow her cover. "Hey, let's find him."

"Who?" asked Roxie.

"Justin!" Katrina said.

"SHH!" Roxie said, her eyes opening wide. "Oh, my gosh. There he is!"

"Where?" Katrina asked as she smoothed out her hair.

Roxie pointed out Justin, who, Katrina had to admit, was a hottie. Well, for a mortal, anyway. She grinned and started toward him, but Roxie pulled her back, saying, "What are you doing? Where are you going?"

Katrina shook her off but, noticing Roxie's shock, patted her awkwardly on the shoulder in what she hoped would be interpreted as a friendly gesture. "Don't worry, Roxie. It's all part of the plan!"

Chapter 4

$\mathcal{S}$abrina walked up to her psychology professor, Dr. Dexter, after class Tuesday afternoon. "Excuse me, but you forgot to call my name during roll call," she said.

"Who are you?" asked the professor, an officious-looking man who, at six feet five inches, towered over his students and almost everyone else in Boston who wasn't on the Celtics.

"Sabrina Spellman," Sabrina said, smiling brightly at her somewhat scatterbrained professor.

"Hhmm," Dr. Dexter said as he glanced down at his notebook. "According to my records, you're not in this class."

"Really. That's strange." Sabrina shifted her books from one arm to the other and explained, "I was last week."

Dr. Dexter stared down at his attendance sheet

and shook his head. "I just don't see your name."

"But—" she started.

Dr. Dexter looked at his watch and cut in, saying, "I'd be happy to help you, but I really don't have time for this today."

"But—" she tried again.

"Although you do look very familiar," he said as he scratched his goatee.

"I answered one of your *Jeopardy*-style questions today. 'Who are Pavlov's dogs?'," said Sabrina.

Dr. Dexter snapped his fingers. "Oh yes! Well done. You should be in this class, you know. Especially since you're doing the reading. No point in just sitting in without getting the credit."

Sabrina took a deep breath and started her explanation over, speaking more slowly this time. "I know, that's what I was trying to tell you. I was in this class up until today. There were never any problems. I was on your attendance sheet last week."

"Oh yes, of course." Dr. Dexter shook his head, finally comprehending the scenario. "Well, I'm sure," he said as he gathered up his things, "it's just some kind of glitch."

"But—" said Sabrina.

"Maybe you should take this matter up with the

registrar," Dr. Dexter called as he hurried out the door.

Sabrina didn't have time to go to the registrar's office just then, because she had French class. As she ran to the language building, a scruffy-haired guy she had never seen before gave her the strangest look, but Sabrina was in too much of a hurry to really think about it. She slid into her seat in the third row just seconds before Madame Steiglitz began to call roll. She went from the names Sarrasin to Taylor, skipping Spellman altogether during her roll call. When Sabrina spoke to her after class, she found out that she'd been dropped from her French class, as well. Sabrina didn't know what to think. She'd rearranged her house according to feng shui principles so that her life would get better, not worse. Sabrina wondered briefly if she should have moved her bed over another inch and a half, or if she should have put the waterfall in a different corner.

Sabrina went directly to the registrar's office and waited in line, wondering what could have happened. Forty-five minutes later she was finally at the front of it, in the midst of a conversation with an unpleasant and multiply pierced work-study student named Bill. He wore dark blue jeans, a black leather jacket, a hoop in his nose, two eyebrow rings above his right eye, and eleven earrings on his left ear. To go with the jewelry, he had a major attitude.

"Hi, how's it going . . . ?" she asked, glancing at his name tag and adding, "Bill."

Bill smirked at her. "Oh, it's you again."

"Excuse me?" Sabrina asked, surprised by the comment because she had never even seen Bill before.

But Bill ignored her second question. " 'How's it going?' What do you think? It's a beautiful day outside and I've been stuck here behind this desk earning minimum wage, answering complaints, dealing with my peers," he said disgustedly. "It's going great. Just fantastic. Now what do you want?"

When Bill opened his mouth, Sabrina noticed that in addition to the piercings on his face and ears, he also had a small silver ball in his tongue. "Wow, did that hurt?" she couldn't help but ask.

"Gee, no one's ever asked me *that* before," he said, twisting up his face in an expression that told Sabrina he was seriously put out.

Sabrina didn't know what to think, so shocked that this stranger was being so hostile. She took a small step back, saying, as sweetly as possible, "Sorry."

The guy behind her in line coughed. Sabrina glanced over her shoulder and noticed three things. One, the line had doubled since she'd been at the back of it, forty-five minutes ago. Two, the guy standing behind her in line had eyes the color of the Mediterranean and the tan of a Greek god. And three, he was smiling at Sabrina in a very flirtatious way.

Sabrina smiled back at him, suddenly deciding that even though she'd been dropped from two classes, at least her day wasn't totally shot. The romance department had been Roxie's focus, but perhaps some of it had rubbed off on Sabrina. They did, after all, share a room.

Bill interrupted her thoughts. "As much as I'm enjoying our little chat, I've got angry people to deal with. Are you just here to annoy me or what?"

"No, I'm here because I have a problem," Sabrina said, turning back and starting to explain.

"Don't we all!" said Bill.

Sabrina decided to ignore his comment and instead she got right to the point. "It seems I've been dropped from some of my classes."

"Is this a joke?" asked Bill.

"No," said Sabrina—once more stunned by his reaction. If she were joking, well, she didn't see how her comments thus far had been very funny. "What do you mean?"

He crossed his arms over his chest and looked her up and down. "I know you," he said suspiciously.

"You do?" asked Sabrina.

"Yes. You were just here yesterday."

"I was?" asked Sabrina.

"You were," said Bill.

Sabrina, not knowing what else to do, decided to play along. "And what was I doing here yesterday?" she asked.

"Dropping all of your classes," Bill answered snidely.

"What?" asked Sabrina.

"You heard me," said Bill.

Sabrina was stunned. She blinked and said, "But, but—no, I wasn't."

"Someone who looked just like you, then. She said her name was, what's your name?" he asked.

Sabrina gulped, and told Bill her name.

"Yes, someone who looked just like you, who called herself Sabrina Spellman, said she wanted to drop all of her classes," said Bill. "Next!"

Sabrina held her hands up and said, "Hold on!"

"No holding," said Bill. "Next!"

Sabrina tried to protest, but Bill was already involved in the next guy's question.

"Did that hurt?" the guy asked.

"Next!" said Bill.

"But I wanted to drop a class," protested the student.

"Then why did you ask about my tongue ring?" Bill barked. "I can't deal with this craziness! Come back when I'm on my break, in a couple of hours."

Sabrina was so upset that all she wanted to do was run home and crawl under her covers. Of course, she couldn't do that. It was 3:00, and she was late for her shift at Hilda's coffeehouse.

She started walking away, but the guy—the gorgeous guy—called after her: "Sabrina!"

Sabrina swung around, wondering how he knew her name, but not exactly disappointed.

"Hey, how's it going?" he asked, jogging up to her.

"Fine," Sabrina said, searching her memory, trying to figure out when she had encountered this guy. He wasn't someone she'd forget. Yet, she had no idea . . .

He didn't notice her hesitation, though. Looking

back over his shoulder, he said, "That guy was way harsh."

Sabrina glanced back at the registration line and shuddered, saying, "I have no idea what his problem is."

He stood there, smiling and expectant, and Sabrina had to ask. "Do I know you?"

He laughed. "That's a good one. Is this your way of trying to get out of our date for tonight?"

"Our date for tonight?" Sabrina asked, truly stunned, thinking, *the feng shui is more powerful than I'd realized!* But before she had a chance to ask, her mystery man was turning to leave.

"Got to run to class, but I'll pick you up at eight, okay?" he asked as he stared into her eyes.

"Eight o'clock," Sabrina said. "See you then."

"Great," he said, flashing her a beautiful smile and turning to go.

"But how do you know where I live?" Sabrina asked.

"You're too much," he said, glancing at her over his shoulder with a laugh.

Who was that? Sabrina wondered.

"Hey you," someone shouted, sounding very hostile.

Sabrina spun around to find herself face-to-face with a security guard. He was a short and stocky middle-aged guy with a thick brown beard and a red face. "Are you talking to me?" she asked.

The guard's blue eyes narrowed in suspicion. "Of course I am. You think you can shoplift and get away with it?"

Sabrina took a step back and said, "I've never shoplifted in my life. Who are you?"

"I was working at the bookstore yesterday morning," said the guard. "I saw you run out of there with the magnifying glass."

"I have no idea what you're talking about," Sabrina said, wondering what was going on.

"Aren't you going to try to come up with something better than that?" asked the guard.

Sabrina threw her hands up in frustration. "I was at home all morning yesterday. I'm sorry, sir, but you've got the wrong person."

He shook his head slowly. "I don't think so."

Sabrina was stunned but, noticing the time, realized she had to be somewhere, fast.

"I'm calling for backup," the security guard said, grabbing the walkie-talkie that hung from his waist.

Sabrina had no choice but to point and freeze him. Once she was safely hidden behind one of the law school buildings, she unfroze him and then took off in a sprint. *What was going on today?*

* * *

Sabrina made it to work in record time, without even using magic, breezing through the door of the coffeehouse at 3:07. Luckily, Hilda was nowhere to be seen.

But Sabrina's sigh of relief got stuck in her throat when she realized she'd just walked into the middle of a nightmare.

Standing in the coffeehouse was someone who looked just like Sabrina. She was dressed just like Sabrina, too—in a standard-issue green apron that said HILDA'S COFFEEHOUSE across the front. But this person was yelling at a customer—something Sabrina would never do.

Sabrina ducked behind an overstuffed couch and watched the scene unfold.

"What are you complaining about?" Katrina yelled at her customer, a young man in a leather jacket, who had curly dark hair covered by a Red Socks cap.

He stammered his reply. "I just told you. I ordered a large latte, and you gave me a small coffee."

"Do you think I care!" bellowed Katrina.

The man stared into his coffee cup and shrugged, saying, "I guess not?"

"Just sit down and leave me alone. Can't you

see I'm busy?" Katrina motioned toward the line behind the man—the line that was getting shorter by the second as customers crept away from the irate and somewhat frightening Katrina.

Sabrina couldn't believe her eyes, or didn't want to, anyway. The last that Sabrina had heard, Katrina Spellman was in an Other Realm prison serving an eternity-long sentence. But here she was taking over Sabrina's shift and terrorizing the customers. What was going on?

An older woman with salt-and-pepper hair pulled back into a ponytail wavered, but then ordered some drinks. Sabrina squinted and got a closer look—only to be horrified by what she saw. The woman Katrina was yelling at was Sabrina's English professor from last semester!

Sabrina stood up, intent on confronting Katrina. But then she saw Morgan waltz into the coffeehouse. Unable to imagine explaining her evil twin, Sabrina quickly turned herself into the first thing she could think of, which happened to be a container of imitation creamer, and hid herself on the condiments table, where she could see what was going on more clearly.

"Hey, Sabrina!" Morgan chirped as she walked through the doors of Hilda's coffeehouse. "What's going on?"

"Nothing," Katrina said, looking around and wondering where all of her customers were. She had an order all ready to serve—an iced coffee and an iced latte, but the customer had disappeared. Was it just because she'd taken the woman's twenty and refused to give her change? Mortals were so touchy, Katrina surmised, as she pocketed the bill. Remembering that she had no mortal money of her own, she opened up the cash register, about to take more.

Unable to believe what she was seeing, Morgan walked straight up to Katrina and asked, "Sabrina, what are you doing?"

Katrina really wasn't in the mood to talk and she didn't know what to do with the cups she was holding, so she poured the iced coffee over Morgan's head.

Morgan sputtered and, wiping her sopping wet hair out of her eyes, said, "Sabrina Spellman! What was that for?"

Katrina smiled evilly and said, "Oh, that was an accident. I'm sorry."

Morgan was so mad, she was shaking and her face was bright red. "An accident? You deliberately poured it on my head!"

"I know," Katrina said, shrugging and grabbing a stack of tens from the cash register. "But I meant to pour the iced latte over your head."

Hearing this, the remaining customers ran out of the coffeehouse, scared that they would soon share Morgan's fate.

Just as they streamed out, Josh walked in. "Hey, Sabrina! Hey, Morgan! Why are you all wet?" When no one answered Josh, he went behind the counter and poured himself a cup of coffee. Although he didn't work at Hilda's anymore, he sometimes acted like he did.

Meanwhile, Morgan grabbed some napkins— which were right next to where Sabrina was hiding—and started drying herself off.

Morgan glared at Katrina in utter bewilderment. "I have a date right after my shift," Morgan screamed. "I just got a haircut and you know it's impossible to replicate a professional blow-dry. And now it's just wasted. I can't believe you did this to me."

Hilda came in from the back room and, with the point of a finger, she stopped time and turned all of the mortals in the room into statues— temporarily, of course.

Hilda turned to Katrina, who had her hand in the cash register.

"What's all the screaming about?" asked a very angry Hilda. "Are you trying to drive the customers away?"

Sabrina transformed back into her human self. "It wasn't me, Aunt Hilda. It's Katrina!"

"I'm not Katrina!" Katrina yelled, pointing at Sabrina. "She is!"

"Huh?" asked Hilda and Sabrina at the same time.

Sabrina had a sinking feeling in her stomach, but luckily it went away when Katrina said, "Oh, never mind."

Hilda made her way toward the evil twin but she wasn't fast enough. In the blink of an eye, Katrina had disappeared. The only trace that remained of her was her evil laugh—a hideous cackle, which echoed through the coffeehouse.

Hilda spun around to face Sabrina, asking, "What is Katrina doing in the Mortal Realm?"

"I don't know," Sabrina said, honestly bewildered.

"Well, I'm going to unfreeze things here, and then we'll go home and figure everything out," said Hilda.

"But what about—" Sabrina was about to ask about Morgan, but it was too late. Her aunt had already unfrozen her.

"Morgan!" Sabrina finished. Turning to her RA and friend, she tried to apologize. "I am so so so so so very sorry. I'm not feeling well. I don't know what came over me. It's like I'm a different person."

"That's no excuse for ruining my outfit!" yelled Morgan. "And you were just stealing cash from the register!"

"What?" yelled Hilda.

Sabrina held her hand up and motioned for her aunt to stop. Then she turned back to Morgan and said, "You're right. But I feel so out of it, and . . ." Here, Sabrina stopped, her mind reeling, trying to come up with the perfect excuse. "I think it's the feng shui," she said feebly.

"Huh?" said Morgan.

Sabrina nodded. "It's the feng shui. After we moved everything around, I just haven't felt the same. It's like I'm out of alignment."

"Morgan, can you take over the shop?" Hilda asked, tearing off her green apron and already heading for the door. "I'm going to see if I can't help Sabrina get back to her old self."

"But I have a date in a few hours!" Morgan said as she wrung out her sopping wet hair.

"I'll be back before then," said Hilda. "And mop that up when you have a second."

"This is so unfair!" said Morgan. But her complaint was voiced to a near-empty room. The coffeehouse door was swinging, and Sabrina and

Hilda were already on their way back to the Spellman home.

The only customer left at Hilda's was Josh, who stared at the condiments counter bewildered and asked, "Hey what happened to the nondairy creamer? It was here a second ago!"

Chapter 5

☆

"How can that be?" Zelda Spellman took off her goggles and stepped away from her most recent experiment. She had been working on finding the right chemical solution that would repair the hole in the ozone layer, but once she'd heard about Sabrina's dilemma, she put her test tubes aside.

"I have no idea how or why, but Katrina is loose in the Mortal Realm!" Sabrina cried.

"And she's sabotaging my business," said Hilda.

"She poured coffee all over Morgan," said Sabrina. "Luckily it was iced!"

"Well, we're lucky she hasn't done more damage than that, yet," said Zelda.

Sabrina remembered her strange day—how her name had been mysteriously missing from her psychology and French rosters; her trouble with Bill the nightmarish guy at the registrar's office; the security guard who tried to arrest her; the scruffy-haired student who sneered at her in the hall on her way to French class—and suddenly the pieces came together, revealing something Sabrina wished she had nothing to do with. "She *has* done more damage. For one thing, she went to the registrar and had me dropped from all my classes."

"Oh dear," said Zelda, who kept a watchful eye on Sabrina's education. She booted up her computer and logged on to the WWW (Witch Wide Web) to see what information she could find. Sabrina and Hilda stood over her, and they all anxiously looked at the screen.

Their concentration was broken by a snide and all too familiar voice. "A family reunion and, as usual, no one invited the cat," Salem said as he waltzed into the room.

"Salem, this is serious. Katrina is in the Mortal Realm and she's ruining my life!" said Sabrina.

"Is that all?" He leaped onto the table where Hilda, Zelda, and Sabrina were huddled in front of the computer.

"Hey, furball, you're in the way," Hilda said, pushing Salem off the keyboard.

But Salem was persistent. "If Katrina could find a way out of prison, something must be going on." He started to get excited. "Maybe they're wiping everyone's slate clean. A new start . . . a new life . . . a way to get out of this cat suit!"

"Don't throw away your flea collar just yet," Hilda cautioned.

Sabrina added, "Anyway, if Katrina was given a clean slate when she was let out of prison, it's already pretty tarnished."

Salem, ignoring all opinions of dissent, darted around the room, frantically shouting, "Well, contact the Witches' Council now! What if they have a limited number of these 'get out of jail free' cards?"

"Please, I'm trying to concentrate," said Zelda. "Salem, if you want Krispy Kremes after dinner, I suggest that you stop bouncing off the walls this instant and keep your mouth shut."

"Sure, play the doughnut card. No one can resist Krispy Kremes—man or cat," Salem said as he hopped back onto the desk.

"Shush!" said Hilda.

Salem glared at her and said, "When I'm back to my old self, you might regret the way you pushed me around."

"Who said anything about pushing?" asked

Hilda, who surreptitiously bumped Salem with her hip, causing him to slide off the table and onto the floor in a jumbled mess.

"So much for a cat always landing on his feet," Sabrina said, laughing.

Salem tried to scrape up a bit of dignity after his fall as he retreated grumbling to the couch.

"Okay, here we are. I have the prison newsletter," said Zelda. "It seems they have a new surveillance system. Web cameras in every cell." Zelda squinted at the screen and then smiled. "Someone named them Max. How cute! There's a link to a demonstration of the system." She punched in some keys, and the computer went black for a second. Coming back to life, it offered a window into cell number 8, where Jezebelda sat alone.

"Hey, how did she get Oreos in prison?" asked Hilda.

"More importantly, do these cameras have something to do with Katrina's escape?" asked Sabrina.

Zelda punched away at the keyboard and returned the screen to the newsletter. "The Other Realm Prison System designed and installed a new computer system."

"Ah-ha!" said Hilda.

"What?" asked Sabrina and Zelda.

"I don't know," Hilda said, shrugging. "It just seemed like a good time to say 'Ah ha.'"

When Sabrina and Zelda gave Hilda a look, she waved her hand and said, "Carry on," completely unfazed.

Zelda turned back to the computer screen and read, "'In updating the files, the new software detected that some prisoners were being held illegally, so they were promptly released.'"

"Oh no," said Sabrina. She sat down on the couch next to Salem, too upset to read further.

Zelda clicked her mouse, and the computer screen revealed a list of prisoners who were sent home. "It says here that Katrina was sent back home to Neptune."

"But Katrina's not even from Neptune," said Sabrina.

"She is according to the new software," said Zelda. "Oh wait, there's some fine print." Zelda enlarged the fine print and read aloud. "'ORPS does not take responsibility for any damages done by prisoners who have accidentally been set free.'"

"It figures. Bureaucracies are the same in any Realm," said Hilda.

Zelda squinted at the screen, adding, "It also

says that to correct any problems, we need to go directly to the courthouse."

"Oh no, not the courthouse!" shouted Hilda.

"Why?" said a panicked Sabrina. "What's wrong with the courthouse?"

"Nothing is wrong with the courthouse, per se," Zelda said, trying to figure out how to break the news gently to her niece.

"There's just always so much red tape at the courthouse, and the lines are unbelievably long," said Hilda. Turning to Zelda, she said, "Remember the last time we were there?"

"You mean the years nineteen twelve to nineteen sixteen?" asked Zelda, shaking her head.

"And to think, we almost missed the Russian Revolution. That would have been a total bummer," said Hilda.

"You were always a sucker for old Trotsky," said Zelda.

Sabrina was beside herself. "It took you four years to get everything straightened out?" she asked.

"Four and a half," Hilda said gravely. "And that was just because we had connections."

Zelda shut down her laptop. "I don't understand how this could have happened. But I'm afraid there's only one solution to this debacle. We've got to go to the Other Realm courthouse and convince them they made a mistake."

The three of them made their way upstairs toward the linen closet, which acted as their portal to the Other Realm. Hilda suddenly turned back, saying, "Be back in a sec. I forgot the scissors."

"Why does she need scissors?" Sabrina asked Zelda.

"We all need scissors," Zelda replied.

"But why?" asked Sabrina.

"You'll see," Zelda said, putting her arm around Sabrina in an attempt to comfort her.

Hilda hopped back up the steps with three pairs of scissors and Salem following close at her heels.

"I want to come," said Salem.

"Salem, I had no idea you were so concerned with my well-being," said Sabrina as she took the scissors that Hilda handed her.

"Whatever," Salem said. "I'm just hoping it's not too late to get in on this computer-glitch thing."

Zelda pointed a finger and zapped Salem back to the couch.

"I mean, I want to help," he yelled.

But he was too late. Hilda, Zelda, and Sabrina were already in the Other Realm—at least Sabrina assumed they were in the Other Realm. All she could see was a wall of red. "What's all this?" she asked.

"Red tape," said Zelda. "Just start cutting."

Sabrina strained to cut through the tape. She heard snipping on either side of her. "Aunt Zelda, Aunt Hilda, is that you?" she asked nervously.

"Yes dear," said Zelda. "There's just about three more hours of this and then we'll be clear."

"Are you kidding?" said Sabrina.

"Don't we wish," said Hilda.

"Can't we magically speed up the process?" Sabrina wondered.

"That *is* the magically sped-up processing time," Zelda sighed.

Fueled by anger and frustration, Sabrina cut through the red tape as quickly as she possibly could. Eventually, she was free and clear.

Sliding the scissors into the back pocket of her jeans, Sabrina found her aunts breaking through at about the same time. *Well, that wasn't so bad,* she thought. *Now all we have to do is find the right person.* But all hope for a quick resolution faded when she saw the courthouse building—well, the building wasn't the problem, it was what surrounded the building. A line. A very long line, which snaked around the building several times.

"This is crazy," Sabrina said, looking around at

her dreary surroundings. "I thought the wait at the Adams registrar's office was bad."

Zelda tapped the shoulder of the person in front of her and said, "Excuse me."

The person in front of the Spellman women didn't have to turn around to answer them, because she had two faces—one of which was at the back of her head.

"Have they told you how long the wait is?" asked Zelda.

"Two years, minimum," said the person. "We're lucky we got here early. At the end of the month, things *really* get crowded."

"Oh dear," said Zelda.

Meanwhile, Sabrina was practically hyperventilating. "Katrina is on the loose, messing up my life. Morgan already hates me. Who knows what else she'll do? I can't wait for two years to fix this problem."

"She has a point," said Hilda. "And I haven't even told you about how she ruined business for me today."

"Okay," Zelda said, looking at her watch. "Sabrina, you go back home and try to do damage control. Hilda and I will wait here and figure out how to fix this mess."

"You will?" Sabrina said, brightening up.

"We will?" said Hilda, who was anxious to get back to work, to make sure Katrina didn't return.

Zelda elbowed her, and Hilda said, "I mean yes, of course we will."

"Thanks, you guys are the best," Sabrina said, beaming as she walked away from the courthouse line. A wave of gratitude washed over her as she got farther from the court. Sabrina felt like the luckiest half-witch alive to have her aunts there to help her. Her relief was short-lived, however, because a second later she remembered the mess that was waiting for her back home.

Having promised to check on Salem, Sabrina went back into the Mortal Realm through the linen closet at her aunts' house. She found the cat at the computer, typing away furiously—or as furiously as he could with only two paws and no fingers.

"What are you doing?" she asked.

"I'm looking for a loophole," said Salem. "If Katrina found one, so can I."

"Oh Salem," Sabrina said with a sigh.

"What? Don't tell me you wouldn't do the same thing if you were in my fur." Salem puffed his chest out at Sabrina, as if to challenge her.

"I'd never be in your fur," she said. "I don't want to take over the world."

"Don't blame me for your lack of ambition," Salem said, turning back to the computer. "Ah, here's the list of released prisoners."

Sabrina looked over his shoulder. "That's a pretty long list," she said.

"So what's one more?" asked Salem. He tried in vain to add his name to the list.

"I'm sure that's protected by some kind of code," said Sabrina.

"And I'm sure if I try hard enough I'll be able to crack it." Salem reached for his glasses and slid them on.

Sabrina rolled her eyes. Salem always put them on when he was getting down to what he called "serious work."

"Just be careful," said Sabrina. "Don't do anything too stupid."

"Shhh," Salem said, ignoring Sabrina's request.

Sabrina walked out the door, but Salem wasn't even paying attention. If he had been, he would have noticed that just as Sabrina was leaving through the front door, Katrina was entering through the kitchen.

"What are you doing?" Katrina asked as she walked up to Salem wearing the most innocent expression she could muster.

"You know what I'm doing," Salem said, not

even looking up from the computer screen. "Didn't I just tell you I need to concentrate? I thought you'd left."

Katrina smiled for real this time, because her plan was working. Salem thought she was Sabrina! "You're on the ORPS Web site," she said as she stroked his fur.

"Of course," Salem said, looking up curiously. "How else am I going to crack the code?"

"The code?" Katrina said, momentarily puzzled.

"Yes, the code," said Salem. "Ow! You're rubbing too hard."

"Sorry," said Katrina, annoyed that she was being ordered around by someone of the feline persuasion, but intent on keeping her true identity under wraps. "What code?"

Salem scowled at Katrina, asking, "Don't you listen to anything I say?"

"Obviously . . . not!" Katrina said, laughing at her cruel attempt at humor. Remembering that she was masquerading as sweet Sabrina, though, Katrina stopped cackling, and asked, "So what are you doing?"

Katrina's laugh had given her away. Salem realized that Katrina was masquerading as Sabrina. He was about to call her bluff when he realized he might be able to benefit from the mix-up. "Is there anything you can do to free me from this cat suit?" Playing off Katrina's desire to cause mischief, Salem added, "I know your aunts wouldn't approve, but what do you say?"

Katrina didn't realize that Salem was onto her. And going against the wishes of Sabrina's aunts did sound like a great new way to cause trouble for Sabrina. She hovered over Salem. "You're on the wrong Web site," she said. "The Witches' Council records are online now, too. You've just got to know where to find them."

"Well, what are you waiting for?" Salem asked, thinking his little plan was going to work just perfectly. "Turn me into a mortal."

Katrina grinned evilly. "Oh, I'll do better than that," she said as she pointed her finger at Salem. "I'll turn you into what you really deserve to be."

Chapter 6

As Sabrina walked into her house near the Adams College campus she tried to brace herself for whatever damage Katrina had caused. She had to come up with some explanation for Morgan. She was leaning toward a temporary chemical imbalance cured by an infusion of chocolate, since it was unlikely Morgan would believe she was suffering from an adverse reaction to bad feng shui—although with Morgan, you never knew. As luck would have it, Sabrina didn't have to deal with all of that just then, because Morgan wasn't home.

"What are you doing sleeping on the couch?" Sabrina asked, staring down at Roxie.

"I'm not sleeping," said Roxie. "I'm trying to sleep. Very difficult, considering."

"Considering what?"

Roxie sat up and pulled her somewhat tangled

hair up into a black scrunchie that she yanked from her wrist. "Considering that our room smells like new paint."

"Oh," Sabrina said, putting one hand behind her back and casually pointing at the room to get rid of the new-paint smell. "Are you sure? Because I painted it yesterday and the windows have been open all night."

"And yet, it stunk all night. I don't know how you slept."

"Guess your nose is more sensitive than mine." Sabrina shrugged. "Let's go check again." She crossed the room and opened her bedroom door. Of course, the paint smell had vanished. Still, Sabrina made a big production of sniffing. "I think it's finally gone," she told Roxie.

Roxie walked into the room, hesitated, and sniffed. "Well, it's not as strong as it was. I guess it's tolerable now."

Sabrina smiled, raised her arms up, and spun around, asking, "What do you think of the rest of the decorating?"

"I like that mirror," Roxie said, pointing to the wall by the window. "But the waterfall is a little cheesy, don't you think?"

Sabrina frowned, saying, "I like the waterfall. It has a calming effect on the whole place."

"Suit yourself," Roxie said with a shrug. She cast Sabrina a sideways glance, trying to put her finger on why Sabrina had acted so strangely the day before.

Noticing Roxie's look, Sabrina changed the subject. "So, it's Tuesday."

"I'm glad that all of this redecorating hasn't made you forget the days of the week," Roxie said sarcastically. "I was worried about you."

"Worried? Why were you worried?" Sabrina asked, suddenly afraid that Roxie had witnessed one, or even worse, more than one of Katrina's antics.

Roxie crossed her arms over her chest and glared at Sabrina with suspicion. "I was just kidding. Where did your sense of humor go?"

"Sorry, Roxie," Sabrina said, relaxing a bit. "I've just been stressed out. It seems . . . it seems there was some bureaucratic glitch in the computer and, as a result, I've been dropped from all my classes."

"Wow, that's so not cool," Roxie said as she sank down onto the edge of her bed.

"Yeah," Sabrina agreed, sitting down on her own bed and leaning against the wall. She wished she could tell Roxie the rest of the story—that the bureaucratic glitch was something that had happened in the Other Realm, something that had led to the release of her evil twin, who was bent on seeking revenge, but of course, she couldn't tell her that. "Anyway, it's not all bad."

"Not all bad? 'Miss Happy and Studious' is dropped from all of her classes and she says it's not all bad?" Roxie asked, leaning back on her elbows.

"I'll get the classes thing straightened out," Sabrina said, thinking back to her aunts stuck in line at the courthouse. "But the good part is, while I was in line at the registrar, I met the cutest guy! And he asked me out."

"So give me the details. Who is he? What's he like? What's his major?"

"I don't know," said Sabrina.

"You don't know?" Roxie said, raising her eyebrows. "Well, what's his name?"

"Um, you know, that's not important," Sabrina hedged, since she really didn't know his name. "What's important is that we did feng shui to focus on romance in here . . . and it worked!"

Roxie, however, was not so enthusiastic, and groaned accordingly.

"So, is it working for you, too? What's the deal with Justin?" Sabrina asked as she pulled one of the many pillows out from behind her back and put it in her lap.

Roxie sighed. "Nothing."

"Well, what have you guys done? Coffee? Made plans for a movie?" Sabrina asked. She'd done the whole romance thing for Roxie's sake, and didn't want to see only herself benefit.

"Like I said, nothing. We talk a little after class, but that's about it," Roxie said.

"Okay. If you like Justin, what's stopping you from letting him know?" Sabrina asked plainly, as if it were the simplest thing in the world.

"So, what—? I should just ask him out?" asked Roxie.

"Yeah, why not? I mean, just this afternoon a guy—a practical stranger—walked up to me, smiled, and just pretended that we had a date. It was a pretty smooth move, and if guys can do it so easily, why shouldn't we?"

"I'll think about it," Roxie said, hoping her answer would get Sabrina off her case.

"Good," said Sabrina.

Just then, they heard the front door slam, followed by Morgan's distinct shriek. "Sabrina! Are you home?"

Roxie looked at Sabrina, surprised, and asked, "What's her problem?"

Sabrina glanced at her bedroom door, which, luckily was closed. "I'll explain later," she said, walking over to the window and opening it up. "Don't tell her you saw me!" she said as she climbed out the window.

Roxie just shook her head. But Sabrina didn't see it. She was already making her way across the front lawn, on her way to the registrar's office, figuring she'd reenroll in her classes first, and then figure out what to do about Morgan. She just hoped her aunts were making progress in the Other Realm courthouse line.

Hilda and Zelda were definitely making progress. They'd moved about half an inch during the past hour. The snail-like pace was taking its toll on their patience.

"What time is it?" Hilda asked, staring at the long and seemingly endless line of people in front of her.

"It's about two minutes later than the last time you asked me that question," Zelda said, feeling equally anxious but in a more composed way.

"So it would be . . . ," asked Hilda, knowing the answer but not dropping the issue, because she felt like annoying Zelda.

"It's two thirty-four," Zelda said primly. "And when you ask again in five minutes, it will be two thirty-nine."

"Oh, okay," said Hilda. She stood up on her

tiptoes to try to see over the heads in front of her. "Can you see the front of the line yet?" she asked.

"No, I couldn't see it three minutes ago, and after moving an entire millimeter since then, I still can't see it," Zelda answered.

"Well, excuse me," said Hilda.

Zelda blinked at her sister. "I'm sorry. I know you're concerned about Sabrina and—"

Hilda interrupted, saying, "Yeah, yeah, yeah, Sabrina will end up fine, but what about the coffeehouse? I've never seen anyone drive away customers faster than that evil Katrina."

Zelda crossed her arms over her chest. "Poor Sabrina's life is being sabotaged and you're worried about a coffeehouse?"

"And Sabrina." Hilda backtracked, feeling a little guilty. "But I'm worried about my business, too. I put a lot of time and effort into the coffeehouse. How about if Jezebelda had gotten free and had taken over one of your lectures?"

"Oh dear," said Zelda. "You don't think that will happen, do you?" She zapped up a pair of binoculars and raised them to her face, looking through them toward the front of the line.

"How should I know? You're the computer whiz," Hilda reminded her sister. "I went to clown college."

"Then why don't you talk to Bonzo? He's at the head of the line," Zelda said, squinting through the high-powered lenses.

"Bonzo Bidderman?" Hilda asked incredulously.

"Yes, Bonzo Bidderman," said Zelda. "Or at least it's someone who looks just like him and has his name painted on the back of his shirt."

"I can't face him," Hilda said, ducking down.

"That's not the same Bonzo who—" Zelda asked.

Hilda nodded her head and took the binoculars from her sister. She stretched up and surveyed the endless crowd in front of them.

"He must be over that by now," said Zelda. "Surely he'd be willing to help you out after all these years. If you explain how urgent it is. If you apologize. . . ."

Hilda shook her head gravely. "It's no use. Bonzo Bidderman vowed never to speak to me again."

"But clown college was hundreds of years ago," Zelda said in protest.

"A Bidderman never forgets," said Hilda.

"How can you be so sure?" Zelda asked.

"Because it says so on the front of his shirt."

"Well, if you don't talk to him, I will," Zelda said, heading toward the front of the line.

Chapter 7

☆

Salem stared at himself in the mirror. Trembling and unable to keep the edge out of his voice, he said, "I think there's been a mistake."

"I don't think so. I think everything worked out just perfectly," Katrina said, smiling at her creation.

"But, but . . . ," Salem quivered.

"What?" Katrina asked impatiently. "You said you were tired of the cat suit."

Salem turned around and looked up fearfully at Katrina, "But you said you were going to help me get back to being my old self."

"No, I didn't," Katrina said, crossing her arms over her chest and staring down at Salem threateningly.

"But, you said . . ." Salem's voice trailed off. "You said you'd turn me into what I deserve to be, and . . ." Salem looked from the mirror back at

Katrina, the truth hitting him like a slap in the face. "Ooh—you really are evil," he said. "And tricky, too!"

Katrina threw her head back and laughed, long and hard and nastily.

Wasting no time, Salem scurried out of the room as fast as he could, although not as fast as he would have liked. Instead of being on the four nimble legs of his former cat-self, he was on four skinny little legs that barely supported his plump body, because Katrina had turned Salem into a rat!

I wonder who will find him first? Katrina mused. *One of the Spellmans, or an exterminator?* Pausing to think about it, she realized either way, it would be funny.

Katrina spotted Zelda's laptop and got another idea. Laughing to herself, she mixed a solution, poured it into a travel coffee mug, and pointed herself back to Sabrina's house near Adams College.

Back in the Other Realm, Zelda ignored Hilda's protests and practically ran to the front of the line. "Bonzo, is that you? Bonzo Bidderman!"

Bonzo turned around as quickly as his oversized clown shoes would allow. Spotting the slender blond woman, he scratched his head, which was covered in bright orange springy curls. He recognized the voice, but wasn't sure from where.

Zelda had no time to waste. "It's me, Zelda Spellman. Hilda's sister."

"Hilda's sister," Bonzo repeated. Now that he realized who she was, the memories came flooding back to him like a powerful tidal wave. Tears welled up in his eyes and then trickled down his cheeks—smearing his rosy red clown makeup. The crying started gradually but, after a few brief seconds, the tears washed down in buckets. Literally. There were buckets at Bonzo's feet overflowing with tears. Zelda had released the floodgates, and now everyone around her in line was ankle-deep in Bonzo's tears.

"Oh dear," Zelda said, staring down at her now-ruined shoes. "Hilda was right." She tried to comfort the hysterical clown.

"Hilda! Hilda! Oh, the name brings back so much pain and heartache!" Bonzo cried.

"Hey Hilda, no cutting in line!" yelled an old-fashioned-looking witch who was standing directly behind Bonzo.

Zelda turned around and looked the witch up and down, scoffing at her broomstick, her tattered black dress, her green skin, and the giant wart on her chin. "I'm not Hilda, I'm . . ." Zelda could barely be heard above Bonzo's wailing. "Oh, never mind, and you don't have to dress that way anymore," finished Zelda.

"Oh please," said the witch. "I was on my way to a costume party last year when I was given a speeding ticket. I've been here ever since."

"I see," said Zelda. "Sorry for the confusion." Noticing that everyone in line was almost knee-deep in tears, Zelda zapped up some super-industrial-sized sponges to soak up the excess liquid.

"Please don't be upset," Zelda said, trying to comfort Bonzo but unable to see why he was reacting so strongly. The incident with Hilda had happened over one hundred years ago. She patted him on the shoulder and said, "There, there."

Hilda came up behind Zelda, her hands on her hips.

"Ahh!" Bonzo wailed, and the tears continued to pour out—now at the pace of a fast-moving water-fall. They accumulated too quickly for the sponges. The angry crowd was soon thigh-high in tears.

"Enough is enough!" Hilda said, holding up her hand. "What happened between us—the incident—it was a long time ago. I'm sorry I ever said it, but I did, and honestly, things probably wouldn't have worked out, anyway."

Hilda's words had no effect upon Bonzo.

"Tell him you didn't mean it. Take it back," Zelda whispered to her.

"It's not going to work," said Hilda. "Anyway, it's not true."

"That doesn't matter at this point. Just try," Zelda insisted.

Hilda took a deep breath. Placing a hand on Bonzo's shoulder, she said, "Bonzo—I was wrong. That bulbous red nose—it is totally you."

Bonzo sniffed. "Really?" he said. "Because I thought of going with the fake one like everyone else, but then I thought, *why*? When the original thing is so much funnier."

Hilda nodded her head gravely. "You're the funniest clown I know. You should have finished first in our class, with any nose you chose."

Bonzo stopped crying in the blink of an eye. The salty flood of tears on the ground dissolved in an instant. Bonzo straightened his bow tie and asked, "So did you hear the one about the penguin, the horsefly, and . . ." Bonzo's voice faded out as he turned and played to the crowd.

"Told you so," Zelda whispered to Hilda as she elbowed her.

Back in the Mortal Realm, Katrina was just exiting Miles's room when she heard the front door of

Sabrina's house open. "Drat!" she shouted as she slammed the door behind her quickly.

"Hey Sabrina," Miles said to the person he thought was his housemate.

"Hi," Katrina said, hiding her now-empty travel coffee mug behind her back.

"What's that?" asked Miles.

Katrina blinked and tried to look innocent. "What's what?"

"That thing behind your back," said Miles.

"Nothing," Katrina said as she inched toward the front door.

Miles looked at her suspiciously. Placing his hands on his hips, he said, "It looks like you were just coming out of my room."

"Really?" asked Katrina.

"Yes," said Miles.

They faced off as if they were involved in some sort of challenge.

"That's funny," said Katrina.

"Yes," said Miles.

They stared at each other. Miles was waiting for "Sabrina" to explain herself, but she didn't. In fact, she was glaring at him nastily, which was way out of character. So much so that his voice wavered when he asked his next question: "So, were you?"

"Were I what?" asked Katrina. "I mean, was I what?"

Miles crossed his arms over his chest. "Were you coming out of my room?"

"No," said Katrina.

"Okay." Miles took a step toward his room, but Katrina moved to the side, blocking his path.

Miles took a step to the left, and Katrina stepped with him, again. "What are you doing?" he asked.

"Nothing," Katrina said, not wanting Miles to go into his room in case her latest potion was still fermenting.

"You know, ever since you brought up this whole feng shui thing, you've been acting really strange," said Miles. "I'm not sure what it is exactly. But I feel like half the time you're a different person."

"Ha-ha! That's funny," Katrina said, sincerely amused.

"Is it?" Miles asked suspiciously.

"Miles, stop being so paranoid."

"I'm not paranoid," Miles argued. "But I'm starting to think you may have some problems. I'll go check my psych text."

"Okay, you do that. Gotta go," Katrina said as she walked toward the front door.

"It's almost four thirty," said Miles. "What class do you have?"

Katrina smiled and said, "Economics."

"I thought you weren't taking that until next year," Miles shouted after her. Miles was technically correct. But he was too late. Katrina wasn't on her way to class. She was on her way to the bank because Morgan wanted to improve her money flow, but she wasn't very specific. Money flowed in and money flowed out. Morgan didn't say which direction she wanted her money to flow, so Katrina would decide for her.

She patted the back pocket of her jeans and smiled. Inside the pocket was Morgan's bank card. And Katrina, with her magic restored to its almost former glory, had no trouble cracking the code.

Miles went into his room and took a nap. Unfortunately for him, he used his pillow, onto which Katrina had just dumped ten thousand microscopic flu bugs.

Had Sabrina known what Katrina was up to, she would have been horrified, but of course she had no idea. In fact, she was in a pretty good mood. She was encountering her first bit of good luck that afternoon when she reached the registrar's office. There were only a few people ahead of her in line, and Bill, the pierced, work-study student, was nowhere in sight. In his place was someone whom Sabrina recognized from her calculus class the semester before, a guy named Joe, who was also the student council vice president.

"Hey Joe, good to see you," Sabrina said, flashing him a bright smile.

Joe grinned, revealing his adorable dimples. His green eyes shined as he re-adjusted his white baseball cap, which covered his short blond hair. "Hi, Sabrina. Can I help you with something?"

"I sure hope so," said Sabrina, who was so relieved by his friendly response. "It seems I've been dropped from all my classes. It's got to be . . ." Her mind reeled as she tried to come up with an excuse. Suddenly, something occurred to her, something that was actually true—technically speaking, anyway. "It's got to be because of some kind of computer glitch."

"Okay, let's see," Joe said as he typed Sabrina's name and Social Security number into the computer.

She watched him anxiously.

He looked at the computer and then back up at Sabrina, saying, "Yeah, you're right. The computer says you were here yesterday, dropping all of your classes."

Sabrina laughed nervously and hoped Joe hadn't been working yesterday when Katrina was there. "That would be a crazy thing to do. I mean, why would I drop all my classes?"

Joe punched some more keys and shook his head. "No worries. It's not a tough problem to fix."

Sabrina was so relieved to be dealing finally with someone who was sane. "Thank you so much for taking care of this."

"No problem," said Joe. He typed something into the computer and then frowned. "But perhaps I spoke too soon."

"What? Why?" asked Sabrina.

"Some of your classes are full," said Joe. Checking the calendar on the desk, he added, "And today is the last day you can drop or add classes."

Sabrina winced.

"You can still get back into them. It'll just take a little work." Joe handed her a stack of green slips and smiled. "You just have to get each of your professors to sign one of these papers, giving you permission to get back into the class."

"Oh, that's it?" Sabrina asked, taking the stack of paper.

"Yes, but there's one more catch. It needs to be

done by five o'clock today. Sorry about this. You know bureaucracies."

Sabrina *did* know bureaucracies, and one always had to allow for the occasional glitch in the system. And being a witch dealing in two Realms just meant that the rule went double for Sabrina. But she couldn't tell Joe about any of that. So she smiled weakly, saying, "Right," as she glanced at her watch. It was already 4:30, which meant that before she did damage control she had to track down six professors in half an hour *and* be back at the office before closing. "Is there any other way to fix this?" she asked.

Joe shrugged sympathetically. "I'm really sorry. You should consider yourself lucky, though. If you'd caught this any later, you'd have a much harder time getting your credits back."

"Yeah, I'm really lucky—evil twin and all . . . I'll have to thank Katrina," Sabrina muttered under her breath.

"What's that?" asked Joe.

Sabrina looked up, surprised that she had actually said her thoughts out loud. *Katrina must really be getting to me,* she realized, shaking her head, attempting to shake off both Joe's question and the stress of the day. "Thanks, just thanks, Joe. You're a lifesaver," she said, forcing a smile.

"I'd better hurry and get those signatures."

"See you," Joe said, waving.

Sabrina was on her way to the language center to find Madame Steiglitz when she noticed something suspicious at the bank—some*one* suspicious, really. Katrina was at the ATM machine on campus, and it looked like she was withdrawing cash.

Once Sabrina had looked around, making sure there was no one she knew in the vicinity—no one who would be suspicious and wonder why she'd never mentioned her identical twin before—she walked up to Katrina. "I didn't know you opened up a Mortal Realm account."

Katrina spun around and, seeing Sabrina before her, narrowed her eyes. "Oh, it's you," she said. "Little Miss Perfect thinking she can improve her life with feng shui."

"How did you know I was into feng shui?" Sabrina asked with a gasp.

Katrina ignored her question, asking instead, "What could you possibly improve in your life?"

"What do you mean?" Sabrina said.

"You already *have* a perfect life," said Katrina.

Sabrina shook her head. "I don't think so. People with perfect lives don't have evil twins bent on sabotaging everything."

Katrina paused before pocketing what little cash Morgan had to her name. "You have a point there."

"So why are you doing this, anyway?" Sabrina asked, trying to keep it cool—a difficult task considering how appalled she was.

Katrina shrugged, saying, "I was bored. It's what I do. Take your pick."

"That's your reason for ruining my life?" Sabrina shook her head, amazed at how frustrating it was talking to Katrina. "I bet I haven't even discovered half of the damage you've done."

"Have you seen Salem yet?" Katrina asked, a smile creeping to her lips.

Sabrina was almost afraid to ask, but she had to. "What did you do to Salem?"

"You'll see. And you're right. You haven't discovered half the damage I've done. And I'm just getting started!" Katrina said. She threw her hands up in a flourish and disappeared.

As Sabrina tried to figure out what to do, her thoughts were interrupted by a beeping noise. Glancing around, she tried to trace the sound to its origin. Her gaze settled on the ATM machine. Katrina had forgotten to take the bank card. Sabrina walked closer and, taking the card out, she read the name on it: Morgan Cavanaugh. Oh great! A receipt was sticking out of the machine. Sabrina looked at it and was horrified once more. Morgan's bank balance read $0000. Katrina had just emptied Morgan's account.

Sabrina groaned, realizing she could only fix onc problem at a time. The clock was ticking, so she ran off to find her professors.

Chapter 8

Writhing and teeming, they were microscopic in size but large in number. An army numbered in the thousands, crawling all over his flesh, covering his body, marching up his ear, over the bridge of his nose, and across his lips. Miles tossed and turned, turned and tossed, whimpered and moaned, moaned and whimpered.

A crash, a bang, and then a bloodcurdling scream woke him from his strange nightmare. Cognizant, yet queasy and drenched in sweat, Miles was confused more than anything. He strained to hear the voices through his bedroom door. They seemed to be coming from the living room.

Someone was yelling. But who and why?

Miles tried to open his eyes. "Tried" being the key word. His eyelids were heavy, and once he managed to open them, a pain shot through his head. Letting out a groan, he closed them again. Opening one eye this time, he looked around. Light peeked in from behind the closed blinds in small slivers—so bright and so strong, they seemed to cut into his mind like a hundred sharp splinters.

Delirious, Miles turned away from the light but the noise continued, so he sat up slowly, because getting up off his pillow took more effort than he'd anticipated. His head felt like it was full of rocks, and his vision was somewhat blurred. He blinked and rubbed his eyes.

Attempting to call out to see what the racket outside his door was about, Miles found he couldn't. His tongue seemed to have expanded to four times its normal size. So weak, it was a struggle to prop himself up on his elbows, but he did just that. Looking around, he tried to adjust to the bright light.

A few seconds later the screams got louder, so Miles, shivering and feverish, forced himself out of bed. With tremendous effort he dragged himself across his room and opened his bedroom door. He looked out into the living room and found Morgan balanced precariously on a chair. "What's going on?" he asked woozily.

"A rat! There's a rat loose in the house!" Morgan shouted frantically.

"A rat?" Miles asked, blinking. The information sank in, waking him with a start; so panicked, he forgot how weak he was feeling and jumped up onto the couch. The fluffy pillows sank, and his knees buckled. Steadying himself by holding out his arms, he looked around and asked, "Where?"

"It was in those couch cushions," said Morgan.

Miles jumped off the couch but landed unsteadily. Stumbling, he crashed into the coffee table face-first. "Ouch!" he said, rubbing his chin. "That's going to be black and blue."

"Who cares?" said Morgan. "There's a rat loose in our house. Someone's got to do something."

Yes, thought Miles. *Someone should do something about the rat. Someone should do something, fast.* He looked over his shoulder and then around the room.

"Well?" Morgan demanded from the chair where she was still perched.

"What?" asked Miles, perplexed.

"Well, do something!" Morgan said as she rolled her eyes.

Miles gulped and said, "Who? Me?"

"Yes, you," said Morgan.

"Why should I do something about the rat?" Miles asked, his voice high-pitched and panicky.

"Because, you know. You're a guy, and guys take care of things like that," said Morgan.

"Well, what should I do?" Miles spotted the four-legged rodent for the first time and shrieked. Loudly.

Both Morgan and Miles were horrified as they watched the rat scurry out from its hiding place under the couch. It's tiny feet tapped against the hard wood as it ran across the floor, straight into Sabrina's room.

"Perfect," said Morgan. She leaped off her chair, ran toward the bedroom, and slammed the door shut. "I just hope he's not big enough to break open the door."

"But what's Sabrina going to do?" Suddenly feeling weak, Miles sank down onto the couch and rubbed his temples.

Morgan, remembering Sabrina's behavior at Hilda's the day before, said, "That's her problem."

"That's pretty cold," said Miles.

"You think that's cold?" said Morgan. "Try getting an iced coffee shower if you want cold."

Miles sneezed and then blew his nose. He felt blood rushing to his head, and the living room felt like a sauna. "Hand me the phone?"

Morgan looked at Miles pityingly and handed him the cordless receiver. "I assume you're calling the exterminator?" she asked.

"Sure," Miles said, willing to agree to anything as long as he got the phone. He called his doctor, whose number was on speed-dial. "I'd like to make an appointment with Dr. Woods," he said to the receptionist who answered.

"You'd better call an exterminator next," Morgan said, before storming up to her bedroom in a huff and slamming the door behind her.

"And who is calling?" the receptionist asked.

"Miles Goodman," Miles said as he felt his forehead. "It's a real emergency. I'm burning up!"

"Miles Goodman," the receptionist repeated. She paused and typed something into her computer. "Is this the same Miles Goodman who was here yesterday?"

"Yes," said Miles. "But that was because I needed to have my toe x-rayed. Now I need to see Dr. Woods for something much more important."

"Weren't you here last week as well?" she asked.

"Yes, that was for my standing biweekly checkup," said Miles. "But something's happened since then."

"And what's that?" the receptionist asked impatiently.

"I have the flu," he whispered.

"May I suggest," said the receptionist, "that you drink plenty of fluids, get some sleep, and try not to call Dr. Woods for at least a few days."

"Wait—" Miles started to say, but he was cut off abruptly and found himself talking to a dial tone. He groaned, and retreated back to his room. "Sleep," he said as he wearily stumbled toward his bed. "I need sleep. . . ." He rested his head on his pillow and was asleep within moments.

Surprisingly, Miles had the same nightmare as before: that there were tiny germs crawling all over his body. He tried to shake them off, but all of his efforts were futile. It was as if they were following marching orders from a source that was too powerful for Miles to combat.

It seemed like just a few minutes but really it was several hours later when Morgan knocked on Miles's door.

Stirred awake, he moaned and shouted, "Go away!"

"Miles, are you in there?" an angry voice called.

"I'm trying to sleep."

Morgan, apparently taking this comment as a cue to barge into Miles's room, did just that. "This is important," she said.

Miles buried his head in his pillow.

"Have you seen Sabrina?"

"Huh?" Miles asked, his voice coming out muffled.

"She must be avoiding me. Probably a smart idea." Morgan stomped upstairs, leaving the suffering Miles alone to wallow.

"Aaah!!!" Sabrina had just pointed herself to her room and stumbled across quite a surprise. Her scream pierced the air.

Sabrina grabbed an umbrella and was about to whack the large rat that was sitting on her favorite pillow when the rat spoke.

"Wait, stop! It's okay. It's me, Salem!"

"What is going on?" asked Sabrina.

"Katrina!" Salem squeaked.

Suddenly there was a knock on her door.

"Sabrina? Are you in there? Is everything okay?" asked a very confused Miles from the other side of the bedroom door. "When did you get home? I didn't see you. . . . This flu must really be messing with my head."

"Sabrina Spellman! Is that your voice I hear?"

Morgan yelled as she came down the stairs and headed for Sabrina's room.

"Oh geez," said Sabrina. She'd barely managed to reenroll in her classes. She still hadn't properly apologized for yesterday's events, and now she had Morgan's bank card in her pocket.

She made a face as she scooped Salem up. Even though he was still Salem, she couldn't help getting creeped out because his feet were so tiny and his tail so long and skinny. He embodied the icky-ness of the rat species so thoroughly, she couldn't help but mutter, "Eew!"

"This is doing wonders for my ego," said Salem.

"I'm sorry," Sabrina said as she shoved Salem into the first hiding place she saw: Roxie's messenger bag, which was hanging on the doorknob. "I can't help it. Stay here. I'll think of something, but first I've got to deal with Morgan."

Chapter 9

Hilda and Bonzo were laughing again like old pals. After the umpteenth recollection of something that had happened in clown college, Zelda had had enough. She faced her sister. "I hate to break up this trip down memory lane, but we're here for Sabrina, remember?"

"Who's Sabrina?" asked Bonzo.

"Our niece," Hilda answered. "She's in pretty big trouble."

"What sort of trouble?" Bonzo asked, taking a big step away from them. "Has she been getting into fights? Holding up convenience stores? Breaking stained-glass windows? Destroying mailboxes with baseball bats for sport?"

Zelda shook her head, saying, "Of course not. Sabrina is a smart, responsible girl. None of this trouble is her fault."

Bonzo rolled his eyes, saying, "Spoken like a true parent."

"Really," said Hilda. "Sabrina is innocent."

"Sure she is." Bonzo's voice dripped with sarcasm.

"But," said Zelda.

Hilda cut her off, waving a hand and saying, "Don't argue with him. You'll never win."

"What's that supposed to mean?" Bonzo asked, clearly offended.

"Nothing, dear Bonzo," said Hilda.

Bonzo was geared up for a fight, but Hilda's words sank in. "'Dear Bonzo'? So you still have some of those old feelings, Hilda? Does that mean you'll consider dating me again?" he asked, honking his horn.

"I can't concentrate on that right now," said Hilda. She sighed and glared at Zelda as if to say, *I told you this was a dumb idea.*

Zelda turned to Bonzo and smiled. "What's your problem with the Other Realm Prison System? Why are you in line?"

Bonzo blinked at Hilda and Zelda, then turned to the courthouse building and scratched his head.

"Why am I in line?" he asked himself.

After a few moments of silence, Zelda glanced at Hilda with her eyebrows raised.

"Well?" asked an impatient Hilda.

"I forgot," Bonzo said quietly.

"You forgot?" asked Zelda.

Bonzo nodded. "I forgot what I was waiting for. It's been a year and a half." He shrugged.

"So much for 'Biddermans never forget,'" Hilda said quietly to her sister.

Zelda broke out into a wide grin and said, "So since you don't know why you're here, that probably means you wouldn't mind if we took your place in line?"

"I guess not," Bonzo said, sighing and stepping aside to make room for Hilda and Zelda. "Until we meet again, sweet Hilda." He took a bow and then waddled away.

"That worked out well," Hilda said a few moments later.

"Don't you feel bad for the guy?" Zelda asked as she watched Bonzo slink off.

"No time to feel bad for the guy," Hilda said, smiling. "We're next."

"Can I help you?" asked a woman behind the complaints desk. She wore a flowing purple robe and a white billowy chef's hat.

"I hope so," Zelda said as she handed the woman the electronic file she'd pointed up when they were still at the back of the line. "It seems there was a computer glitch and our niece's evil twin has been set free."

The woman opened up the folder. Inside was a twenty-first-century version of a crystal ball. It displayed, on a very clear liquid display screen, Katrina's shenanigans that Sabrina had witnessed.

Zelda, Hilda, and the purple-cloaked woman watched Katrina sabotage the sales at the coffeehouse and empty out Morgan's bank account.

"My, she's been busy," the woman behind the counter said sympathetically.

"It's truly awful, isn't it?" Zelda said, horrified herself at the extent of the damage Katrina had caused.

"I'll bet those customers of mine will never be back," said Hilda.

Ignoring Hilda's comment, the woman handed Zelda back her file and said, "I feel horrible for your niece. I'm so sorry. I do hope she can get her life back together and figure out a way to get her evil twin back into prison. It's obvious her release was a mistake."

"I'm so glad you think so," Zelda said, relieved.

"Now what can I help you with?" asked the woman.

Hilda and Zelda looked at each other, and then back at the woman behind the counter, perplexed. Zelda was speechless, so Hilda said, "We thought you could help us. That's why we've been waiting in line for so long."

"You've been waiting in this line because you want to talk to someone about a prisoner?" asked the woman.

"Well yes," Zelda said plainly.

"But this is the line for traffic complaints."

"You're kidding," Zelda said, regaining her ability to speak and hoping that the woman was in fact joking.

"Oh dear," the woman said, shaking her head so vigorously that her chef's hat slid down to her eyebrows. "I wish I were kidding. But the line for computer glitches is next door. And it's longer than this one."

"Longer than two years?" asked Zelda.

"A bit," the woman said sheepishly.

"How much longer?" asked Hilda, her voice raised to a pitch of near-hysteria.

"The last I heard, the line stretches out to almost six years," said the woman.

"Six years," Zelda repeated. "Oh dear."

"Almost six years. But you don't have to wait in line," said the woman.

"We don't?" Hilda asked hopefully.

"No, you just have to take a number."

Zelda and Hilda walked up to the machine that was spitting out numbers and took the first one they could.

Reading their slip of paper, they both looked forlorn. They got number 8,975,243. Currently, the court was calling number 6.

"Poor Sabrina," said Hilda.

"I wonder how she's doing," said Zelda. She opened up the file folder once more and pressed a button so it showed what Sabrina was presently doing in the Mortal Realm. She and Hilda huddled around the screen and watched the scene unfold.

"Sabrina!" Morgan yelled as she pounded on the door furiously with one hand and rattled the door-knob with the other.

The very frazzled Sabrina realized she had been ignoring Morgan's angry calls for too long. She turned toward her bedroom door and pointed, unlocking it and causing Morgan to come in so quickly, she almost fell over.

"Hi, Morgan," Sabrina said brightly.

Morgan regained her balance and said, "Don't you 'hi' me." Her green eyes narrowed into angry slits as she peered at Sabrina. "What was that stunt you pulled at the coffeehouse yesterday?"

"What stunt would that be, exactly?" Sabrina asked, stalling for time.

Just then, Roxie came into the room. Sabrina sighed in relief, until she realized that Roxie didn't seem very happy with her either.

"What's wrong, Roxie?" Sabrina asked, not only because she was concerned, but also because she hoped to deflect Morgan's angry line of questioning.

Roxie flicked her hair over one shoulder and said, in a voice obviously meant to mimic Sabrina's, "'Just ask him out.'"

"What?" said Sabrina.

"Your advice," Roxie said nastily. "Brilliant, really. Just go up to Justin and ask him out for tonight."

"So you did?" Sabrina asked weakly, with a sinking feeling in her stomach.

"I did," said Roxie. "And he said I was too late. He already had a date."

"Ouch," Morgan said, now distracted.

"I'm so sorry, Rox," said Sabrina. "But try to look on the bright side."

Roxie and Morgan both glared at Sabrina. "What bright side?" they both spit out.

"Um . . ." Sabrina realized that she'd spoken too soon. She tried smiling at her housemates, but they wouldn't budge. "At least you tried," she said, shrugging.

"Whatever," Roxie said, flicking one hand in the air dismissively.

"I so totally agree with you," said Morgan.

Roxie picked up her messenger bag and started to open it up.

"Wait a minute!" said Sabrina.

"Ah!" yelled Roxie, throwing the bag out the window.

Sabrina cringed and covered her face with her hands.

Roxie stood still as the color rapidly drained from her face. Her arms were pinned down straight against her sides, and she looked totally freaked out.

"I know your bag is a little out of style, but all of your stuff is," said Morgan, who was staring at Roxie, puzzled. "Why such a violent reaction?"

Frozen and pale, Roxie was unable to snap back with a clever put-down.

Sabrina looked up. "What is it?" she asked, with feigned innocence.

"There was a rat in my bag," Roxie managed to stammer.

"I've already called the exterminator," said Morgan. "There's no need to worry."

Salem grunted after his not-so-soft landing. Scurrying quickly out of the messenger bag, he darted into the bushes. Hiding and trembling, he felt kind of strange. His whole body was warm and tingly. He looked down at his tiny paw and noticed that it was swollen. His whole body was transforming, mutating into something else. Salem, assuming that Katrina's rat formula was temporary and he'd be returned to his normal cat self, was relieved, but only for a brief few seconds. Once he saw the feathers, he knew that things would be downhill from there. . . .

"You called an exterminator?" asked Sabrina, horrified.

"I am the RA—which right now stands for 'Really Angry,' but that's not the point. Apparently I'm the only one who can get anything done around here."

Sabrina ran to her window and looked out. The messenger bag lay flat on its side, empty of all contents. She grimaced, wondering how she was going to find Salem now. She hoped he hadn't gone far.

"Ah-hem," said Roxie.

Sabrina turned around and faced Morgan and Roxie, who were both glaring at her. What did they want? An explanation or an apology? They deserved both, but Sabrina didn't know where to begin. Stalling and taking a step backward, she said, "Uh."

"This I've got to hear," said Morgan.

"First of all, I'm so sorry. I can explain everything. Really, I can," Sabrina said as she inched toward the bedroom door. "I just can't do it right now." She bolted for the door and ran out, slamming it behind her and pointing one finger over her shoulder to lock it. She raced across the living room, out the front door, and to the side yard, under her bedroom window. Once there she caught her breath, then pointed her finger again, letting Roxie and Morgan out.

And then she searched for Salem. She couldn't find the rat anywhere. But strangely, she did find a chicken, who, in a familiar voice, squawked, "Help me Sabrina!"

Chapter 10

Hilda and Zelda paced back and forth in front of the new line—which was set up like a deli counter but, instead of meats and cheeses, there were judges in long dark robes, taking complaints, answering questions, and solving problems.

"Sabrina's life is falling apart and they're only on number eleven," said Zelda.

"There's got to be another way to talk to a judge," Hilda said as she looked around at the hordes of people waiting. "Clown college wasn't this much of a circus!"

"Do you see any other ex-boyfriends with lower numbers?" asked Zelda.

"Very funny," said Hilda. "I meant there has to be a way to get to see a judge faster. This is an emergency! You have three PhDs. Can't you think of something?"

"I'm trying, I'm trying," Zelda said, suddenly noticing a very plump chicken. "I'm sure we can at least cut in in front of the poultry."

"Geh!" squawked the chicken, causing Hilda and Zelda to look twice and see Sabrina.

"You've got to help me," Sabrina said, picking Salem up and putting him into Hilda's arms.

"We already ate lunch," Hilda said, holding Salem away from her as far as her arms would extend, and wrinkling her nose.

Salem squawked and said, "This isn't lunch. This is your favorite former cat. Please, I'm begging you—help me!"

"What are you doing in the Other Realm, dear?" Zelda asked, putting her arm around Sabrina.

"I had to get some help. Katrina is too much for me to handle. She stole all of Morgan's money, and she turned Salem into a rat who then turned into a chicken."

"You've got to do something," Salem wailed. "I'm afraid to see what comes after chicken."

"Things are just crazy," Sabrina continued. "Miles is sick. Roxie's love life is going worse than usual, and I can't help! I don't know what to do."

"Did you get back into your classes?" asked Zelda.

"Yes," said Sabrina. "It wasn't easy to track down all of my professors, but I managed. I just hope Katrina doesn't figure out that I'm fixing the mess she's made."

"Where is she now?" asked Hilda.

"I don't know," Sabrina said, throwing up her hands in frustration. "That's the worst part."

"Well, we can check out her latest antics here," said Zelda. She opened up Sabrina's high-tech file, which showed Katrina at the cafeteria again. She had six sandwiches, a pepperoni pizza, two cheeseburgers, and three milk shakes in front of her. She was flanked by stacks of cookies— chocolate chip on her left and gingersnaps on her right.

"Another few hours and she's not going to fit into her prison uniform when she gets back in there," said Hilda.

"*If* she gets back," said Sabrina. Squinting at the image on the screen, she said, "Hey, she just dripped pizza grease on my brand-new peasant blouse!"

"She turned me into a chicken and you're worried about her messing up your clothes?" asked Salem.

Sabrina was so frustrated by how helpless she felt, she didn't know how to answer. She tried to turn Salem back into a cat, but she couldn't undo Katrina's spell. She hoped her aunts could bail out the poor feline.

"Dare I ask how this happened?" asked Zelda.

"Some sort of computer thing," Sabrina explained. "He thought she was going to change him back into human form."

Salem looked sheepishly out from half-lidded eyes.

"So you knew it was Katrina and you went along with her plan?" Zelda accused more than asked.

Zelda took Salem from Hilda and examined him. "You say you were a rat first?" she asked.

"He's always been kind of a rat," said Hilda.

Salem pecked Hilda on the shoulder and cried, "Kick me while I'm down, why don't you?"

Zelda shifted Salem to her other arm and then glanced at her watch. "I think I know the spell Katrina used on you, and if I'm not mistaken, then it's—"

"Oh no," Salem cried, trembling because of the familiar tingling feeling overtaking his body.

"It's going to happen again," Zelda finished.

They watched in horror as Salem's chicken body mutated again and he shrank into a parrot.

"What a pretty bird," Sabrina said, marveling at

Salem's bright orange, green, red, and yellow feathers. "Can we keep him?"

"As if we had a choice," said Hilda.

"I should really get him back to the Mortal Realm," Zelda said, placing Salem on her shoulder. "Do you think you two can handle things up here?"

"But what about Katrina?" asked Sabrina. "Running damage control is a full-time job." Looking around and suddenly noticing the boisterous crowd around her, she asked, "How are things going here, anyway?"

Zelda shook her head, and Hilda groaned.

"What?" Sabrina asked, bracing herself for the worst.

Hilda glanced up at the screen that displayed numbers and told Sabrina, "We have about 8,500,003 people ahead of us in line."

"You're kidding!" Sabrina said with a gasp.

"Do I look like I'm kidding?" asked Hilda.

"Uh-oh," said Zelda, who had glanced down at Sabrina's file once more and was watching Katrina in action.

"What now?" asked Sabrina.

"If I could determine some sort of pattern, it might be easier to come up with a solution," said Zelda. "Something tells me these acts aren't random."

"Well," Sabrina said, starting to blush. "I do have an idea about that. I mean, where Katrina got her ideas and everything."

"Really?" said Hilda.

"Well, what is it?" Salem chirped, fluttering his wings.

"Last weekend I went to a lecture on feng shui, and I think that maybe—" Sabrina stopped speaking when she noticed her aunts smiling at each other. "What?" she said.

"I remember when feng shui was just learning how to walk," said Zelda.

"He was an adorable baby," said Hilda. "It's a shame he turned into such an egomaniac. He just had to be a household name."

"I think you're both thinking of the wrong feng shui," said Sabrina. "This is the decorating philosophy. You know? Improve your life by reorganizing your house. Work on the five elements and . . . oh, never mind. Look, Katrina was obviously listening somehow when we each decided what element of our lives we wanted to improve. Let me think." Sabrina strained to remember, wishing she had her notebook with her. "Morgan wanted to improve her money flow, so that's why Katrina emptied her bank account."

"That's awful," said Hilda.

"You know what's worse?" said Sabrina.

"That I'm the one who could really use the money," said Salem, whose feathers were ruffled, literally and figuratively.

"No," said Sabrina. "That I'm going to get blamed."

"Shut up, Salem," said Hilda.

"If Morgan presses charges, it will drastically cut down on my social life. Not to mention limit my career choices," Sabrina said, adding, "which is what I was focusing on."

"And that's why she had you dropped from all of your classes," said Zelda.

"I never would have thought that Katrina could be so methodical," said Sabrina. "I mean, you've got to respect how she really went out of her way to ruin not just my life, but the lives of those I love."

"It's no excuse for turning me into fowl," Salem chirped.

Sabrina ignored Salem. Turning to Zelda, she said, "I do have Morgan's bank card. After emptying the account I guess Katrina didn't see any use for it." Sabrina reached into her back pocket and pulled out the card.

Zelda held out her hand and said, "I can take care of the bank problem if you give me that. How much cash do you think Morgan had in there?"

"I have no idea," said Sabrina.

"I'll figure it out," said Zelda.

Sabrina smiled. "You're the best, Aunt Zelda. Thank you."

"She's the best?" asked Hilda. "Who's going to stick around here and make sure I get to see a judge?"

"You're both the best," Sabrina said. "I'm the luckiest half-witch alive."

"Before we go back to the Mortal Realm, though," said Zelda, "why don't you tell me why your life needed improving?"

Sabrina was stumped, but she had to say something—Hilda and Zelda were waiting for an answer. "I don't know," she said truthfully.

"Are you unhappy with school?" asked Zelda.

"No, school is great," said Sabrina. "In fact, I'm really enjoying my classes this semester."

"Are you having problems with your housemates?" asked Hilda.

"No. Everyone has their quirks, but basically it's a lot of fun," Sabrina answered.

"Well then, what's the problem?" asked Zelda.

Sabrina shrugged. "To tell you the truth, I don't even remember."

"I think we'd better go back to the Mortal

Realm," Zelda said. "We're running out of time."

"And I'm running out of life-forms," said Salem.

Zelda ignored Salem's comment. Turning to her sister, she said, "Hilda, we're counting on you."

"I'll do what I can," she said. "I just hope it's enough."

"It'll have to be," Sabrina said, following Zelda through the fray of already cut red tape.

"Get cracking, ladies! Caw! Caw!" ordered Salem, surprised when a parrot noise came out of his beak. "Oh, excuse me," he added sheepishly.

Sabrina and Zelda arrived back at the Spellman house with parrot Salem in tow. Zelda pointed to an empty space by the staircase, and a cage with a small perch appeared. She placed Salem in, gently.

"What, no birdseed?" he asked.

Ignoring Salem, Zelda pointed up her home laptop and interfaced it with the one she'd had in the Other Realm. "If I could just figure out what Katrina did to Miles." Turning to Sabrina, she asked, "What was he focusing on? In your little feng shui redecorating plan."

"Health," said Sabrina.

"Health," said Zelda. She noticed her laptop was not where she had left it, and that there was residue in one of the beakers. Zelda put on her glasses and picked up the beaker. "And the opposite of health is—"

"Miles," said Sabrina.

"Because he's always sick," Zelda said, half to Sabrina and half to herself. She placed a sample of the green liquid onto a slide and put it under the microscope. Bending down to examine it, she muttered, "Hmm."

Sabrina walked over to Zelda and peered over her shoulder.

"Your breath is fogging up the lens," said Zelda.

"Sorry," Sabrina said, taking a step back. "But I think it's usually in his head—Miles's colds and flu and everything."

"Not this time," Zelda said as she looked up from the microscope. "This time it's real."

Chapter 11

"**W**hat are you doing sneaking around in my room?" asked Miles, who had just come home to find Sabrina closing his bedroom door.

Sabrina hid her travel coffee mug behind her back and tried to come up with an excuse, fast. "Huh? Me? Coming from your room? I wasn't coming from your room." Armed with a chemical solution to heal Miles, Sabrina was in fact coming from his room. She had dumped half of the contents of the coffee mug in Miles's bed, and now the trick was to get him to drink the rest of it.

"Yes you were, and that's the second time, I think," said Miles.

"What were you doing out? I thought you were

sick," Sabrina said, trying to change the subject, and actually curious. She was surprised that Miles was well enough to be up and dressed—albeit badly dressed—in a pair of orange cords, brown sneakers, and a navy blue hooded sweatshirt. Even when he wasn't legitimately ill, by the early evening he was often in pajamas or old sweat-pants.

"The doctor's office," Miles said, sitting down on the couch, picking up a magazine, and leafing through it.

"How did it go?"

Miles sighed and said, "Not so great. Dr. Woods refused to see me, so I had to go to some-one new. And the person she recommended had very cold hands."

"And this was bad because . . . ?" Sabrina asked as she sat down next to him.

"It just was," said Miles. "These things can't al-ways be explained, but there's something about shaking hands with someone and if their hands are too cold, it's just never a good thing."

"Uh-huh," Sabrina said. "And I thought my aunts were the only crazy people in my lives."

"Speaking of crazy, have you noticed that there's something really strange in this house," said Miles.

"What do you mean?" Sabrina asked, wondering what else Katrina could have done.

"Well, we've never had rats before. And don't get me wrong, I'm not complaining, but the exterminator came and said he couldn't find anything. Not even a dropping or a trace of a rat, no excess fur or footprints, or holes where there might be a nest. Morgan and I saw one, though."

"Maybe it was someone's pet hamster or something who got lost, and you just thought it was a rat," Sabrina offered, trying to get him off the subject.

"Maybe," Miles admitted. "But there's more. I've been having wacky nightmares—wackier than usual, that is. And then of course, there's you not acting like yourself."

"I'm not?" asked Sabrina. She clutched Miles's shoulders and, shaking him a little, asked, "What do you mean? How am I not acting like myself? When did I see you last? What did I do to you?"

"Whoa," Miles said, staring at Sabrina as if she were possessed. "Do I have to check the basement for pods again?"

"Sorry," Sabrina said, trying to act normal again. She didn't want the entire house to think she was out of her mind. Plus, she still had to convince Miles to drink the healing potion that Zelda had created. She pasted on a smile that was so fake, it hurt her cheeks. "I guess I overreacted. I, uh, had a lot of coffee this morning. So what else is bothering you?" she asked.

"I've just felt that for the past few days, the house has been falling apart."

Sabrina was overcome by a wave of guilt. If she had never introduced the feng shui ideas, Katrina wouldn't have been armed with information about her housemates' weaknesses. Of course, that wouldn't have stopped her evil twin from wreaking havoc, but it may have slowed her down enough for Sabrina to discover her sooner. Miles wouldn't be suffering the way he was now, with a legitimate flu. He'd have some sort of made-up one, which was probably more comfortable— well, not for the other housemates, but at least for him.

"How's your flu?" Sabrina asked, sincerely concerned.

Miles sighed and said, "Horrible."

Sabrina held up her coffee mug. "I have something to confess, Miles. You were right. I was in your room a little while ago. But it's only because I was looking for you."

"Why?" asked Miles.

"I have this medicine to help your flu. It's sort

of an old family remedy," she said hopefully as she handed Miles the mug.

He opened up the lid and peered into it. "It's green," he said.

"It works miracles," said Sabrina. "It'll heal you, I promise."

Miles swirled the liquid around in the mug. "Really?"

Sabrina paused, trying to come up with the words to convince him. "It's like magic," she said.

"I suppose it can't make me more sick that I already am," said Miles. He cocked his head back, raised the liquid to his lips, and drank it all down.

Sabrina smiled, relieved that something was finally working out the way she wanted it to.

"Blech!" he said, after swallowing the last gulp. Wiping his lips with the back of his hand, he added, "That's the worst thing I've ever tasted. Even worse than my mom's brisket, and that's saying a lot."

Sabrina cringed. "I'm so sorry, Miles. I'm sorry you had to get sick. This will work. I promise."

Miles shrugged. "If you say so," he said, not sounding at all convinced.

Just then there was a knock at the door. Roxie came out from her bedroom and walked through the living room. Noticing Sabrina and Miles talking on the couch, she asked, "Isn't anyone going to get that?"

Sabrina glanced toward the door and realized that it was eight o'clock and she had a date with a stranger.

Roxie answered the door with Sabrina behind her, following close at her heels. The guy, whatever his name was, was gorgeous. He was wearing faded khakis, and a blue sweater that brought out his eyes and reminded Sabrina of the sea.

Roxie stood there staring at him, stunned. "Justin," she said. "Did you change your mind?"

Sabrina felt a sinking feeling in her stomach. Of course it was Roxie's friend Justin! Katrina had struck again. Sabrina cursed herself for not realizing it sooner.

"Roxie, what are you doing here?" asked Justin. Shifting awkwardly from one foot to another, he stared past Roxie at Sabrina. "I'm here to pick up Sabrina."

"What?" asked Roxie.

"This is not as bad as it seems," said Sabrina.

"It's not?" asked Roxie.

"Can you excuse us for just a minute?" Sabrina asked as she closed the door.

With daggers in her eyes, Roxie glared at Sabrina and asked, "What is up with you?"

Sabrina shook her head. "This is all wrong. You're supposed to go out with him. I think you should just answer the door and tell him it was a mix-up."

"What?" said Roxie. "Do you think I'm a total loser? He's here to pick up you!"

"Not for long," said Sabrina.

"What are you talking about?" asked Roxie.

Thinking fast, Sabrina said, "Really, this was all part of my plan. I said I'd go out with him here because I was afraid you wouldn't tell him how you felt. So, now that he's on your doorstep, you've got to make your move."

"That's the dumbest thing I've ever heard," said Roxie.

Maybe it is, thought Sabrina. *But it's got to work.* Pointing her finger, she froze everyone in the house, then went outside to freeze Justin. Staring at him, she thought for a minute. Then she pointed at him and recited the following spell:

"Justin with blue eyes so bright,
You came to this doorstep on a certain plight
To pick up a blonde, but she's not who you think.
She's two-faced, schizophrenic, and sort of a fink.

Roxie's the one you'd rather date.
Show some interest tonight before it's too
late.
When I unfreeze you now, the sparks they'll
be flying,
Because without Roxie's company you'd be
a-crying."

After casting her spell Sabrina went back inside and unfroze everyone. "Just trust me," she said to Roxie, pushing her toward the door.

"I'll answer the door, but I doubt I'll ever be able to trust you again," Roxie said.

"Sabrina, are you ready? I—" Justin started, but cut himself off when he looked at Roxie. "Roxie. Wow. You look. Amazing." He spoke slowly, as if each word were an entire sentence. "You are amazing."

Sabrina ducked out of the house fast. Pretending to wipe the sweat off her brow, she said, "Have fun you two!"

Chapter 12

☆

"*Presto recover-o,* with this spell may Salem serve out the rest of his sentence in the Mortal Realm as originally planned—in the form of a common house cat."

With a poof of smoke, Salem morphed into a chicken, then a rat, and finally, back into a cat. "YEEE-OOWW!" he screamed. "You couldn't go straight back to cat?"

Zelda crossed her arms and glared at Salem. "You're welcome," she said sarcastically.

"All of this changing from fur to feathers is exhausting! I need a nap," Salem said, settling down in his favorite spot on the couch. As he curled up he noticed that his tail was long and skinny like a rat's. "Uh, Zelda, you're getting a little sloppy here."

Zelda raised her eyebrows in response.

"You call this a silky cat tail?" asked Salem impatiently.

"You can't try to outsmart the Witches' Council and get away with it completely unscathed," said Zelda.

"But how did they . . . ?" Salem didn't bother to finish the question. Zelda's honesty, not to mention her tattletale tendencies, were legendary.

"I'll give you back your tail in a few days. I don't want you to forget your mistakes just yet."

"Oh, come on," said Salem.

"Do you want the rat body back to go with the tail?" Zelda asked.

"I won't say another word," said Salem.

"As if that's even a possibility," said Zelda.

Salem raised his head. He was about to protest, but realized he couldn't.

"Anyway, what about Sabrina? There's still work to be done," Zelda reminded him.

Right on cue, Sabrina burst into the house. She noticed Salem feigning sleep on the couch. "Oh good. I'm glad he's back to normal. Er . . . well, almost," she added when she noticed his tail.

"You won't be glad for long," joked Zelda. "Just wait until he opens his mouth again."

"Miles is feeling better. Your flu solution was amazing. Roxie is out with Justin. Now, what about Morgan? I know she's still mad at me after the Hilda's coffeehouse incident, but am I going to be a convicted felon, too?"

"No, everything is fine," said Zelda. "I managed to get the money back. The bank manager is quite a handsome man. I wish it had been harder to convince him of the mistake. We could have chatted longer." Zelda handed Sabrina Morgan's bank card.

"You can give this back to Morgan when you get home."

"I'll tell her I found it at Hilda's," Sabrina said as she pocketed the card. "And that she must have dropped it at work. Hopefully, she'll be grateful enough to forgive me for the coffee Katrina dumped on her."

"One thing at a time, Sabrina. Speaking of Katrina, she's still on the loose," said Zelda.

"I wonder how Aunt Hilda is doing in the Other Realm," said Sabrina.

"I know a good way to find out," Zelda said as she started to climb the steps. "Are you coming?"

"Of course," said Sabrina. "What else would I want to do tonight? Not go out on a date with some gorgeous guy."

Zelda gave her a warning look.

"Who is just perfect for Roxie," she covered.

"It'll be much more fun to chase around my evil twin."

The Other Realm Courthouse line was twice as long as it had been when Sabrina and her aunts first went there. But Hilda was almost at the front.

"We're almost up!" she said, jumping up and down and waving her number, which was suspiciously much lower than it used to be.

"What happened?" asked Zelda.

"I managed to get a lower number," said Hilda.

"How?" asked Sabrina.

"It's not important," Hilda answered. "Oh, but Zellie, if a large, hunchbacked man named Quasimoron shows up at the house and says you're his prom date—"

"HILDA!" Zelda bellowed so loudly, it shook up the people at the end of the line.

"Hey, did you want to get this thing resolved or what?" asked Hilda.

"No, you're right. If it will save Sabrina," Zelda said calmly, smiling at her niece.

"Don't worry, you'll be doubling with me and Quasi's brother. They're really a lot of laughs. Too bad they're only two hundred and twelve."

"Hilda, they're so young," Zelda exclaimed. But she had no more time for protests.

"Number 104!" called the judge.

"That's us!" Hilda said, pushing her way to the front of the line. "Hello, your honor," she said.

"Hello. How can I help you?" asked the judge, a huge man in a bright blue robe.

"There's been a mistake," said Sabrina. "My evil twin was set free from prison because of a computer glitch."

"Oh, I see," the judge said, nodding his head. "Was this a mistake because of the computer system switch?"

"Yes, that's exactly it," said Zelda. "How did you know?"

"Well, that mistake was fixed hours ago," he said.

"Excuse me?" Hilda said, suddenly upset.

"The mistake was fixed. There was a recall. All prisoners who were released have been automatically sent back to prison," said the judge. "Now, if you'll excuse me, I have an important meeting to get to."

"Do you mean I've wasted an entire afternoon in line for nothing?" Hilda said.

Sabrina and Zelda looked at each other and smiled.

The judge took off his robe and revealed golf clothes. He put on a visor and then reached for his clubs. "Catch you ladies later," he said, waving over his shoulder as he strolled away.

"Unbelievable!" said Hilda.

"Let's take a look, just to be sure," Zelda said, flipping open her file. They all watched Katrina, who was unhappily back in her prison gear. Together again, she and Jezebelda were eating Oreos and counting the bricks in their cell.

Zelda handed Sabrina the file. "Why don't you hang on to this for a while, just to be safe."

"Will it protect me from Morgan, who totally hates me now?" asked Sabrina.

"I'm sure you'll manage to smooth things out at home," said Zelda.

Suddenly there was a loud honking, shouting, growling sort of noise. "Hilda!" They all turned to where the racket was coming from. Bonzo and three large panda bears were making their way clumsily toward the Spellmans. "Since you've got the rest of the night, how about a walk down memory lane?" Bonzo called so loudly that the crowd of people turned to look at them. "I brought the pandas!"

"Oh, what the heck," Hilda shrugged.

"But what about the coffeehouse?" Zelda asked.

A lightbulb went off over Hilda's head, literally.

"Hey Bonzo, how would you and the boys like to go to the Mortal Realm?"

Bonzo honked, and the pandas did a dance, which Hilda took to mean yes. "Great," she said. "Follow me."

As the Spellmans made their way back to the portal to their linen closet, Hilda whispered to Zelda and Sabrina, "It's the perfect way to get my customers back. A free circus!"

"That'll be nothing compared with the circus at my house once Morgan, Roxie, and Miles get hold of me," Sabrina said.

Chapter 13

"**S**abrina!" Morgan yelled. "What are you doing in my room?"

Sabrina was caught off guard, and it took her a few moments to recover. No matter, though: Morgan was waiting for an answer and was blocking Sabrina's path to the staircase. Surely she wouldn't let her pass until she had an answer.

"Listen, Morgan. I'm really sorry about how I treated you at the coffeehouse," Sabrina said, meekly tucking a strand of hair behind her ear. "I don't know what came over me."

"So you've said. And the strangest part is, it's not even the nuttiest explanation you've come up with," Morgan said, rolling her eyes.

"I feel so bad about ruining your hair, I really wanted to make it up to you. So, I got you an appointment to get it redone. My treat!"

"That's so nice!" Morgan said. "And after the last few days, shocking."

"You're such a great RA and friend. I just wanted to let you know." Sabrina coughed, hoping that the excuse she'd prepared didn't sound like too much of a long shot. "I think I was just really thrown off by this feng shui stuff. It was like I was a different person. I couldn't stop acting weird and doing awful things."

"It happens, although you *were* acting weird. Even for you," said Morgan.

"But it's all over now," said Sabrina. "I've realized that my life is pretty great as it is. I think Miles is right: Feng shui is a powerful force, and it shouldn't be messed with by mortals, I mean, by people who aren't experts. I'm back to normal, and I'm going to move all the furniture back. I'm so sorry. It'll never happen again."

"I'm so glad," Morgan said, giving Sabrina a hug.

"Me too!" said Sabrina. "I just hope Roxie's not still upset."

"I think she's too distracted to be upset," said Morgan.

"Really?" said Sabrina. "You mean distracted because of Justin?"

"Uh-huh. I'm kind of bummed that I didn't

snatch him up myself . . . but well, I guess there's always next year."

Sabrina shook her head, too happy that things were back to normal to give the don't-steal-your-roommates'-boyfriends lecture.

Walking back downstairs, she began to move the furniture back to how it was before she'd decided to "feng shui" her life.

Miles came home just as she was pushing the couch back to its old spot.

"Are you feeling better?" she asked him.

"Well, my flu is cured," Miles said as he flopped down on the couch and picked up the remote. "But I sprained my ankle just a few minutes ago."

"That's too bad," Sabrina said, happy that life was back to normal.

Miles flipped to the sci-fi station then glanced around the room. "Something is different around here. It's the furniture—it's all back to where it used to be."

"Yeah," Sabrina said, wiping the sweat off her brow.

"I thought that was bad for our energy flow," said Miles.

Shrugging, Sabrina said, "You know, Miles, I think we were all doing pretty well before I went feng shui crazy. I just can't believe it took turning everything upside down to figure out the meaning of the saying "If it ain't broke, don't fix it."

"No, it's not broken, just sprained," Miles said, fully absorbed in the *Planet of the Apes* episode and not really hearing what Sabrina said.

No matter, it was my lesson to learn, Sabrina thought.

Going into her bedroom, Sabrina pointed her finger, bringing the walls back to their old shade of eggshell.

Next, she cleared away all of her feng shui props. Well, all but one.

Sabrina still kept the mirror in her room—she had learned a few things from her experience with feng shui. Although rearranging the furniture wouldn't improve her life, she did have to keep on her toes. She'd pay closer attention from now on. She wanted to know who was entering her life and why, because there was no telling what could happen otherwise.

About the Author

Leslie Goldman was born in Philadelphia, Pennsylvania, and raised in Los Angeles, California. She received a master's degree in anthropology from the London School of Economics and, like all anthropologists, moved to New York City to write fiction. So far she has written over thirty books for children. She is allergic to nontalking cats and has several aunts, none of whom are witches.